THE SAINT OF THE
DRAGON'S DALE

THE SAINT OF THE DRAGON'S DALE

WILLIAM STEARNS DAVIS

"And he wist not that his face shone."

EXODUS xxxiv. 29.

WILDSIDE PRESS

THE SAINT OF THE DRAGON'S DALE
William Stearns Davis

PUBLICATION HISTORY: July, 1903,
as part of the Macmillan Little Novels series.
REPRINTED, Wildside Press, 2004.

Published in the United States by
Wildside Press
P.O. Box 301
Holicong, PA 18928-0301

www.wildsidepress.com

ISBN: 0-8095-0067-1

TO

LE BARON RUSSELL BRIGGS

AN EVER KINDLY
FRIEND AND COUNSELLOR
TO ME
AS TO SO MANY OTHER
SONS OF HARVARD

CONTENTS

CHAPTER I
JEROME OF THE DRAGON'S DALE

PATTER, patter,—the rain had beaten all day on the brown roofs of Eisenach. The wind swept in raw gusts across the rippling ocean of pines and beeches which crowded upon the little town from many a swelling hill. Under the grey battlements the Horsel brawled angrily. At the Marien Gate, Andreas the warder dozed in his box, wrapping his great cloak tighter. He had searched few incoming wagons for toll that day. It was very cold, as often chances even in summer in tree-carpeted Thuringia. Andreas was sinking into another day-dream, when Joram, his shaggy dog, having opened one eye, opened the other, then started his master with a bark.

"Hoch! hold!" cried Andreas, rubbing his eyes. "Who passes?"

"Johann of the 'Crown and Bells.'" And the warder saw the tow-thatched stripling of the innkeeper tugging a great basket, whilst his buff coat dripped with rain.

"And whither away?" quoth Andreas, settling back, as Joram ceased growling.

"The 'Saint' in the Dragon's Dale needs his basket, rain or no rain—curse him!" And Johann's broad mouth drew into no merry smile.

Andreas crossed himself as became a pious Christian. "Do not blaspheme the Saint. Ask his prayers rather. This is a noble time for the gnomes and pixies to go hunting in the Marienthal for just such blithe rascals as you. So pray hard and run harder."

Small need of this. Gnomes and pixies had been much in Johann's mind since goodwife Kathe, his mother, had thrust the basket on his reluctant arm, and haled him by an ear to the inn door. It was nigh as bad as wandering by night, to thread the forest on a day like this. As he quitted the gate, from east, west, south, was pressing the green Thuringerwald,—avenue on avenue of stately beeches, lofty as church spires, graceful as the piers of some tall cathedral. He could see their serried, black trunks running away into distance, till his eye wearied of wandering amid their mazes. A clearing next, fresh chips, young weeds, a carpet of dank leaves—but the wood-cutters were gone. Then the path opened enough to give one glimpse to the westward and southward, toward the leafy peak of the Hainstein; and beyond and higher, to a proudly built castle,—with a scarlet banner trailing through the rain,—the Wartburg, one-time fortress of the Landgraf of Thuringia, now the hold of Baron Ulrich, boldest and wickedest of all the "ritters" who watched the roads in these evil days which had fallen upon Germany.

The glimpse of the Wartburg cheered Johann. Man was there—and what was a "robber-knight" beside a redoubtable pixie? Likewise, what likelier place for pixies than those glades just before? Johann had not forgotten the wise tales of old grandame Elsa; and there it was,—the stone cross, where forty years ago the griping burgomaster Gottfried had been found lying stiff and cold, with purse untouched, and never a scar, save a little one behind his ear."He had gone to meet the Devil, and the Devil had stolen his soul;" so said Father Georg in church. It was heresy to doubt it.

Johann was sure it was best to pray at the cross. He plumped on the wet grass, said two Aves and a Paternoster. At the last"Amen," whir!—went something off behind. A gnome? No; only a partridge. He trudged on happier. Now the glade was narrowing; the trees thickened, the brook sang over rocks and sands. One could see the slim trout shooting in the pools. Johann's stride lengthened. The forest closed all view. He crossed the stream on stepping-stones, and drew a long breath."Only two hundred paces more!" It had ceased raining, but all the trees were hung with pearls, and shook down showers at every sweeping breeze. The air was suddenly grown warm. The last hundred paces, Johann seemed walking into a sheer wall of rock, whence the stream crawled from under a tiny fissure. What dwelt beyond—dog-men who fed on babes, or only ordinary and commonplace devils, Johann did not care to guess. Ten paces from the precipice he halted, crossed himself as a precaution, laid down the basket, and turned to a sapling whence dangled a rusty helmet by a leathern thong.

Thrice he beat with a stick, and the metallic booms sent new quakings, not appeased by a voice which proceeded from the centre of the beetling rock.

"Who is this that comes to the Dragon's Dale?"

"I, Johann of the 'Crown and Bells';" and Johann's teeth rattled.

"Have you brought the basket?"

"Surely, holy father; bread and cheese as always on the first of the month."

"Christ then abide with you and your good parents. In the helmet you will find the accustomed payment. Now leave the basket and depart."

From the helmet Johann took a silver piece,—a strange coin current amongst the Orient infidels. However, silver was silver; it came from a holy hermit, and Johann's chief need was a swift gait home; so home he flew, his teeth a-chattering.

For long after his going, absolute silence held the glade; then seemingly out from the precipice emerged a man who walked straight to the basket and lifted it so easily as to convince a grave crow—the sole onlooker—that here was a mortal of wondrous strength. The new-comer moved in long strides which did not belie the mighty proportions of thigh and limb. Over his broad shoulders, scarcely bowed with fast and age, hung a brown sheepskin jerkin, sewed with thongs, descending below the knees and bound with a bit of rope. Feet, neck, arms, were absolutely bare, hairy, and sinewy. How the face looked one might not tell, all hidden as the features were behind the unshorn snow-white hair and beard which veiled almost everything save two marvellously lustrous blue eyes.

Without a word or look to right or left, he lifted the basket, and strode directly toward the rock. Not till the wall was arm's length away could a stranger have discovered how one boulder thrusting before another opened a passage, narrow, tortuous, dark, betwixt the masses of sandstone. The defile was scarce wide enough for two to pass. Underfoot trickled a shallow stream. The stone walls were mantled with green moss and myriad ferns and harebells. Often the rocks locked closer, throwing the gorge into twilight, or opening, disclosed the grassy hill-slopes fifty feet on high. The solitary went onward, heedless of gloom, until, after following this uncanny path for nigh two hundred yards, the rocks sprang apart, and as by art-magic the long-prisoned sun burst forth, and shot his glory over the greenwood. Instantly all the beeches' leafy clusters were glistering with diamonds, the sheen of the grassy slopes grew dazzling, the brook flashed on its way, with a rainbow in every ripple, whilst right over the massy Wartburg hung a true"Bow of the Promise" in foil splendour.

The stranger mounted the slope, till castle and hills were clear in view; then spoke his first word.

"O dear Lord Jesus Christ, if this Thy present world is fair, how fair must be Thy heavenly world, before which all this shall flee unclean away!"

The speech was not German, but some strange tongue of the East, alien indeed to this northern forest; but the hermit only scanned the sky and valley once, then pressed up the hillside until in a hollow shaded by immemorial pines, and carpeted by their brown needles, there was a hut of wicker and of boughs, and from the damp wood before the entrance a stream of thin smoke crawled upward, whilst at the crunching tread of the hermit a beast started from the dying fire, growled softly, and wagged a bushy tail,—a yellow, white-toothed wolf, who raised his black muzzle to the basket, and mildly sniffed for bread, beseeching with low whines. But the strange man only spoke two sharp words, in the same Eastern tongue.

"Down, Harun!" And the wolf slunk back to the fireside to switch his tail and eye the basket timidly.

The hermit deliberately entered the hut, soon to return with a cake of coarse black bread. Again the wolf started, but the man rebuked him.

"First, we must thank God."

The man knelt by the fire, and the beast regarded in silence.

"We thank thee, O Father of all mercies, for food and for another day of life in which we may prove ourselves repentant of our sins, and more obedient to Thy will, *sic oramus in nomine nostri delecti Domini, Jesu Christi: Amen.*"

The "Amen" was answered by a yelp; the wolf rose on his hinder legs. The man broke the cake into halves scrupulously equal, and cast one to the beast who caught it with his teeth, growled gently, and began to devour. His master seemed in no haste to eat. It lacked an hour of evening. The slant sunshine through the trees streamed in a witching brightness. The air grew warm. From the pines bird answered to bird. The man went across the narrow clearing, drew from his girdle a keen knife, and cut a notch upon a sturdy fir. Many notches were there already, some long, some short, forming a kind of reckoning. He scanned them carefully, clearing the moss from some with his fingers.

"Eight years ago, eight years lacking one month,"—he was speaking in the same uncouth tongue—"this same day

14

I had to quit Fulda for this place. The Abbot wished to make me esteemed a saint, and so draw pilgrims to the abbey. About this time I was assailed by the Demon of Spiritual Pride, and thought myself somewhat righteous. Then might I have fallen into his clutches and been burned forever, I and the soul of my Sigismund, but I escaped him, *gloria Tibi, Domine!*"

The wolf had finished the cake, and gave a low whine to attract attention.

"You may go," spoke the man, upraising his head, whereat the beast shambled away into the forest, and his master returned by slow steps to the fire.

"Eight and thirty years ago to-day? ah! what was it then? Mother of Christ, I can remember,"—there shot a gleam out of those wild eyes which made them like bright sparks,—"it was the fête at Naples. Frederick the Great, the 'Wonder of the World,' was there. With the French Count of Autun, and the Flemish Seigneur of Charleroi, I held the lists against the best lances of Sicily, of Italy, of Spain. None unhorsed us, but I did best. They led me to the Emperor; Mathilde crowned me. That night she and I walked together in the gardens, and saw the moon upon the shimmering sea. It was that night she said,—"

A convulsive tremor shook his frame. He dashed his hands against his breast as if to tear his heart forth from its covert. The words were nigh a cry.

"Oh! all will come back. I cannot banish it. The fiends are strong, strong! That day I slew the Aragonese, Don Filipo, in his sins. He forgot to confess ere he rode to the tourney. At the Judgment bar I must answer for his soul, for twenty more. O dear Lord Christ, I am too weak! I cannot endure it!

I am lost forever!" He passed his hand across his forehead as if to brush a mist from his eyes. "My head reels. Yes, I kept from sleep. I ate nothing yesterday. But prayer and fast will not beat the demons I away. I have been to Rome and to Jerusalem. *Cui bono?* Would God I dared lie down and die. But die I dare not, for I must redeem your soul, my Sigismund, my son."

He looked longingly upon the bit of bread. The fast had been long, even for that man of iron. Nevertheless, he shook his head.

"Man may not live by bread alone. Let me first reward my evil memories with the lash that they may fear to return to torture me."

He hastened inside the hut. A bed of pine boughs and of furze, a coarse blanket, a water-pot, and above the bed a great silver crucifix and a brazen plate, whereon some Byzantine had graved a stiff Madonna and the Blessed Child—this seemed all the furnishing. But from beneath the bed, he took a short leathern scourge, its three lashes plaited with round balls of lead,—no toy, though swung by a girl. Slipping aside the sheepskin, he laid the lash with steady hand upon the naked shoulders. At the first whistle the red welts leaped out, at the second the blood, but under his great beard the strange man only smiled grimly. "It shall be forty stripes save one," had been his vow, and the lash whistled on, whilst he uttered two names at every blow, "Jesu! Sigismund! Sigismund! Jesu!"

Then suddenly the scourge sank. Human feet were sounding on the piney carpet. Then a voice, not his own, was calling him by name.

"Jerome! Jerome of the Dragon's Dale! As you love our

Lord,—out!"

And to discover this unwonted intruder, Jerome donned his sheepskin, and issued forth in haste.

CHAPTER II
WITCH MARTHA

NOW as Jerome quitted the hut, he saw neither man nor maid, but only two huge, black ravens, which flew to his shoulders, as to a familiar perch; whereat the one on the right, cocking his glossy wicked head, croaked out a doggerel couplet:—

> "Good Christian, look out!
> The Devil's about!"

To which his mate made instant answer with still saucier quirk of head and bill:—

> "Ho, he! Never fear!
> I'm Satan! I'm here!"

Jerome crossed his breast, but he did not thrust these blasphemers off. Nevertheless a shrill voice from behind a great black fir commanded sharply:—

"Zodok, Zebek,—sons of Beherit and grandsons of Lucifer,—back, both of you, and fear the sign of the cross."

Whereupon with a whir, sudden as that which had brought them, the inky pair were gone toward the summons. Jerome had fixed his beetling eyebrows upon the black fir tree.

"Martha, you child of Perdition."

"Here, and very much at your service, *Sanctissime*," came back the feminine voice, half mocking, half respectful.

"Saint me no saints, or if my curse avails with God or angel, you receive it. What brings you again, witch and necromancer, abhorred by all save the Father Devil?"

"*Benedicte*, thanks to you for such sweetness. Well, I have a work for you more pleasing to God than scourges and fasting."

"Work from you? Can any good thing come out of you, O spawn of Beelzebub?"

"'Can any good thing come out of Nazareth?' ay, so the Jews said, and mayhap quite rightly." Here all the glade reechoed with a long shrieking laugh, whilst Zodok and Zebek croaked gleefully.

But Jerome's great head had sunk upon his breast.

"*Mea culpa, mea culpa;* who am I to cast the first stone against this woman?"

"Well," demanded the shrill voice, "may I come forth?"

"Come forth."

And with a rustle there came from her shelter a woman—but what a woman! For her head would have risen only to Jerome's breast, but her girth nigh equalled her height, or surpassed it. She had a weazened pock-marked little face, a very small mouth, still smaller black eyes, an exceedingly shrewd, upturned nose, and when she spoke her teeth shone white and sharp as Harun's. Black was her kirtle, black the kerchief which trailed over grey locks and over shoulders, black her shoes when they peeped from under her dress, but Jerome (had the hermit an eye for such vanities) would have said that those feet were very small, and the hands small, too, and white,—hands which many a princely dame in Goslar or Hildesheim would have done well to envy. The ravens sat on either shoulder, winking their sinful eyes and waiting new chance for croaking.

Jerome's attitude was sufficiently unconciliatory. He made not the least sign of greeting her.

"Have I not bidden you to come no more?" was all that he demanded.

The small nose turned itself up in derision.

"You have."

"And have I not eschewed all the world, abandoned myself these many years to solitude and austerities, such as my weak flesh can bear," and the hermit sighed modestly,"and yet you approach to tempt me? A man would be sufficient emissary from Satan, and you—a woman—"

Again the greenwood rang with laughter.

"O Lord Jesus Christ! run, tell Thy Father He made a sad mistake, when He made us womankind. Jerome of the Dragon's Dale is wiser! He knows we are only fiends let loose from hell."

"Silence, sorceress! declare your errand, and briefly."

The witch looked at him out of her little eyes with a sly quirk, very like that of Zebek.

"Ulrich of the Wartburg—" began she.

"A sinful man even amongst sinners," assented the hermit.

"Has been on a raid."

"He has done the like before; God assoil him—which I very much doubt."

"And he has taken a prisoner."

"Our Lady soften those beasts' hearts that they demand a reasonable ransom. Ulrich commonly slaughters."

Martha looked on the hermit more keenly than ever. "Hark you, Jerome of the Dragon's Dale; the prisoner is no man to put to ransom, or to meet his doom with brave brow. Ulrich has taken a little maid."

"Jesu!"—Jerome crossed himself.

"And she is nobly born,—a wisp of a girl, a lamb amongst worse than wolves."

The hermit stared hard.

"How know you this? Ulrich has been a king of fiends, and all his men apt vassals for their master, yet he has always stopped short of whithering off women. He has sought purses, not prisoners of that kind."

Witch Martha took a step nearer. "How do I know it? Well—to a sheep-eyed Eisenach lad I might say I bestrode my crook, and Zodok and Zebek grew forty fold larger, and flapped me up to the Wartburg on their backs. But since I speak to a saint, a man who has never known blood, nor sin, nor passion,"—Jerome winced at the irony but did not rebuke her,—"I will say this. First, I was in the thicket by the road below the Madelstein, and saw our noble baron riding home with his prey; second, because Anna a poor wench at the castle has just come to me for a philter to charm back a laggard lover. And so I got the whole story."

"But the maid?"

"Is noble, I tell you, yet scarce a child of twelve. They slew all her company. For after Ulrich had bidden to 'stand and un-sack,' he grew frightened, for he found he had stopped too great folk to let them go their ways, too great to put to ransom. So it was out swords, and trust that graves in the forest will tell no tales. Only the maid he spared."

"For what end?" demanded the hermit.

"For what use are women put in such dens as the Wartburg? Perhaps Priest Clement cried out for her. But praised be St. Nicholas,—she is over young for him!"

"I must pray," quoth Jerome very deliberately.

"While the angels weep, and God our Father wonders why he has spared you so long from burning."

"Why that reproach from you, woman?"

"He! ho! Our Saint has still his pride, because if you were a *ritter* with twelve-score *lanzknechts* it would be a crying sin to be so nigh the Wartburg, and never wing a shaft for rescue; while you, the Saint of the Dragon's Dale, who have the power of seven *ritters,* mock God by saying, 'I must pray,' and leave Ulrich to work out his evil will."

Jerome stared still harder.

"I am a man of peace and vowed to the works thereof."

"And to Ulrich of the Wartburg is not the little finger of a saint thicker than the loins of a *markgraf?*"

"Saint? Have I not commanded—?"

Witch Martha threw up her little hands, while her fat body swayed with laughter.

"Oh, think yourself Satan's twin brother if you will! But you know all Thuringia calls you the 'Saint of the Dragon's Dale,'—and just because you will keep yourself aloof and see but three men in a twelvemonth your fame grows. Ay, this very night there will be five hundred souls from Gotha to Meiningen who will add, *'Sancte Uieronyme Eisenachæ ora pro nobis'* after they have petitioned St. James and Our Lady."

"These things must not be;" the hermit's forehead was almost turning white.

"These things *are!* and Ulrich and all his crew, if they love saints little, fear them much. Therefore go to him boldly and demand from him the maid."

"And if he refuse?" pressed Jerome.

"He will not refuse, yet if he slay you, are there no glories for the martyr?"

The hermit took a step toward her.

"I will go."

That was all he said. As he approached she moved back noiselessly, as by some occult power; her round little body seemed to glide,—not walk. In an instant she vanished, with only Zebek's hoarse call to die away in the depths of the forest.

> "Ho, he! Never fear!
> I'm Satan! I'm here!"

Jerome went into the hut, and drew from beneath the bed a long, heavy staff with a formidable brass head,—the wood exceedingly hard, and carved with quaint letterings of the East. Swung in trained hands such a weapon was no mean match for a halberd or broadsword; yet Jerome sighed as he lifted it.

"I go on a good work; nevertheless, it nigh seems looking back with the hand long set upon the plough; God pity me, yet—" here he swung the great staff about his head till he heard the air a-singing, and the sound seemed sweet as music; then he crossed himself, as extra talisman against such carnal joy, and went down into the Dragon's Dale.

* * *

The evening had been settling fast. All the clouds above the western hills were painted rose and gold, the gold fading, the rose deepening. Above the eastern Drachenstein rode three pale stars—nigh blotted by a broad white moon. The wind had sunk to a whisper, to which the woods were answering. The stream purled slumbrously as Jerome emerged from the Dragon's Dale; from the clearing he sent one glance westward and north to the Wartburg, where Ulrich's blood-red banner still trailed to a redder sky, then with swift, strong strides he plunged into the heart of the forest. Blind was the path, and ever darkening; it wound over stock, stone, through glade and hollow. Now he heard the delicate hoofs of the red deer as they scampered in dread of some poacher; now the moonlight made a silver foot-cloth down broad avenues of cedars whereof the planter was God alone. Still the hermit bore on, fearless, tireless, no forest beast more certain of his way, until the blind path circled upward, the trees again were opening, and upon the sheer height against the gloaming reared the grim Wartburg, defiant, scarce approachable, but shooting from loophole and window red shafts of light, whilst on the soft night air drifted the scream of coarse song and coarser revel.

"I go to fiends, not men;" so spoke Jerome, and halted a

moment to pray, then boldly moved forward. In an instant he entered the light of a camp-fire; a half-dozen low-browed men with steel caps and clattering halberds leaped from their dicing on the grass, barred his path with oaths, and demanded:—

"Your business?"

"And yours, friend? Who are you to ask?"

"To ask, quotha? Has not Ulrich set us here to watch the road, while the rest have wassail and women in the castle? Selfish swine! But now who are you?"

"A sinful man."

"We're all noble fat sinners here; but that's no pass-word."

"I come on a holy errand."

"Hoch! I'm just the scoundrel to halt an angel, or even to test the thickness of his head!"

Down crashed the halberd, but the staff flew up to meet it. The *lanzknecht* scarce knew how, but his weapon twirled out of his hands and whisked over into a thicket. Miracle or magic,—this strange being's power was dangerous. The six recoiled toward the fire, then as the flame glittered across the hermit's face with one accord that evil crew sank on knees,—cheeks white, teeth a-chattering.

"The Saint! The Saint of the Dragon's Dale. Woe! *Miserere!* We are damned!"

But Jerome, without a word, went up the long way to the Wartburg.

CHAPTER III
MAID AGNES

GOOD cheer at the gate, more cheer in the bailey, in the great hall of the Wartburg the blithest cheer of all. On the brass fire-dogs in the cavernous chimney tall flames leaped from the snapping logs; in their wall-sockets the red torches shook at every gust from the open loopholes. The polished oak of the ceiling, the green and crimson scrolls of the frescos, the sheen of the long black benches, the glister of the gold and silver drinking-horns, the brightness of the pictured tapestries,—all these joined in a scene of barbaric splendour. Upon the dais, under the arched recess, Ulrich, "Free-baron by the Grace of God," and master of an hundred men, sprawled half his length in his arm-chair, banged his great scabbard on the floor, and swore that he was in just the mood to fight My Lord the Emperor.

Michael the Breaker, the black-haired giant who sat on the lower stool at his suzerain's side, capped the oath by wishing the King of France and the Holy Father at Rome were foes too, just for furnishing merry sword-play. While amongst the men-at-arms and brutish women who were fast getting wilder over mead and beer, Priest Clement—

the jolliest sinner who ever pattered a mass—lolled on his bench, called for another pot of the smacking Erfurt beer, and dared man or demon to deny that his was the happiest life in all the world.

"*Veritas! veritas!* true was the saying my wise mother taught me!"

"And that wisdom, Father?" snickered Ruprecht, who was then tying a new knot in his dagger-strap to keep reckoning of the man he had killed that day.

> "For a happy time once, then a fowl you must slay!
> For a merry long year, don't your wedding delay!
> For a lifelong carouse, then a priest you must stay!"

So Clement; but Ruprecht growled sullenly,—

"We are less fortunate than your reverence; it is Friday, but can we have no dispensation for a side of ham?"

"*O malefice!* Unfaithful shepherd have I been to my sheep that such impiety should spring up in their hearts even as a wish! Have you no fear of God's Judgment?"

But here the beer came, and Clement's nose went into it. Ulrich was pulling his great carcass up into the chair and squinting round the room.

"The maid? where?" he demanded.

"The prisoner?" asked Michael, his vizier.

"The same;" and Ulrich's eyes went over into a dark corner behind the fireplace, then his orders sounded sharp as a cracking lash.

"*He!* Franz-of-the-Ram's-Pate, bring her this way."

A great man-at-arms, whose strength lay in muscle not in wits, bestirred himself and dragged from the shelter a girl whose slender form seemed sinking from his hands as from the touch of flame. In the wavering torchlight few might look upon her face; yet that she was merest child one quick glance told, and all could have seen the evil grin of My Lord Baron as he surveyed her.

"So *this* is the prisoner?"

The girl, too scared or too brave for sobs, remained absolutely still. Ulrich continued his inquest.

"Had she no jewels nor rings?"

"The most reverend Father Clement, possessed himself of them," ventured Franz, to be cut short by a hurried *'Maledicte!'*from the priest, and a warning from Ulrich that the holy man's share, when the spoil was divided, should be abated accordingly.

"Well, girl," continued the Baron,"and who may your gallant father be, that you travelled from Bamberg with so handsomely furnished a company? Some fat burgomaster of Hamburg or of Lubeck, I dare swear by Saint Godehard's self!"

The girl held up her head now, and her voice was very shrill.

"I am come from the convent at Bamberg, where the Lady Abbess reared me, and I go to Graf Ludwig of the Harz, who is my father."

Had the prisoner suddenly become a knight in mail, Ulrich could scarce have liked this answer less. He stormed out a fearful oath"not to lie," which only drove her back to silence, and every feaster stopped his drinking. The Baron looked uneasily on Michael.

"Does the wench lie?" he demanded.

"I could see from the first that she was nobly born, by her

small hands and feet, and she is too scared to lie. She is Ludwig's own brat, as I am a sinner."

"Holy Trinity!"swore Ulrich, staring hard;"this is what comes of setting on companies one knows nothing about. You see she is but a puling child, though tall for her age, and of no use to us. Ludwig of the Harz! He will pull down the Wartburg stone by stone, but never pay a ransom. I know him. Safer to rouse a she-bear just missing a whelp!"

"Ludwig may never know to blame us," suggested Michael;"those other fools are too dead for babbling. There are more bands who 'live by the stirrup' betwixt Goslar and Bamberg to share the suspicions."

"But you dogs will wag your tongues in the Eisenach taverns," frowned his lord."Stories will fly; the Graf swoop down."

"Then the wench is best—" but here Michael drew a big finger across his thick throat and laughed.

"Back with her, Franz!" thundered Ulrich, losing temper."She is too white now even to whimper. I will question her more in the morning, when my crown does not buzz. Fill me the tallest horn, and you, Priest Clement, roar out a tune to hearten us!"

The girl vanished in her corner. The news that they held so unwelcome a prisoner had dampened the jollity of all save the holy priest, but he held his mug high, opened his huge mouth, and made the rafters ring.

> "Horse, lance and away,
> Man nor fiend shan't us stay,
> Though to the Black Pit we're a-flying!
> From a mug and a maid

> To a merry mad raid,
> That's the best way for living or dying!
> "Let a clumsy monk howl
> To the saints from his cowl,
> As he shrinks on the straw at Death's creeping.
> To the tune of the brand
> Let us die as we stand,
> And we'll leave to base varlets the weeping!
>
> "So be blithe through the night,
> And by day ride and fight,
> That's the lanzknechts' brave life, I'm a-saying!
> *'Yo, ho, he! Yo, ho, he!*
> *Neath the greenwood spur we! '*
> *So all the deep war horns are braying."*

The last lines were blared as a chorus out of forty throats, the rafters shook, the torches quivered. Silence then, an unwonted step, varlets with long faces rushing, Baron Ulrich twisting in his chair, Priest Clement turning red, the door tapestry parting, and strange eyes looking in upon that wanton crew. The raiders were face to face with Jerome of the Dragon's Dale.

* * *

Well for Jerome that he had mastered the Demon of Spiritual Pride! Ulrich of the Wartburg, ruler of one hundred of the wildest spirits in Thuringia, had cowered behind his silver-lace doublet and tried to look fierce, but vainly. Michael the Breaker remembered a prayer his mother had taught him. Priest

Clement's wriggling tongue was still as a fire-dog. When Jerome stood before the dais and bade Ulrich deliver up the prisoner then and there, My Lord Baron turned all ashen under his bronzed skin and asked what would be the consequences if he did not, only to understand that obstinacy now would advance him farther yet into Heaven's ill graces. It had all ended before an onlooker could have counted an hundred.

"Give him the maid, Franz, and all the fiends go with her!"

So ordered Ulrich, and Franz complied whilst his great knees beat together and his ill-deeds stared large at him. Some cried "Blessing!" "Absolution!" others. One of the wicked women knelt and kissed the skirt of the sheepskin as Jerome swept out with never a word to them all. That the feast flickered out in silence and trembling sobriety, there is small need to tell.

But Jerome led the little maid through the wide courts, where other revellers cast timorous eyes on them, under the spiked portcullis (where the warder was crossing himself on his corselet) out into the black span of the night, with only the stars and the moon and the wind to bear them company.

As for the maid herself, it had all been one whirling dream since noon, when the Baron's men had stopped her escort under the greenwood. Happy was she, in that she was too young to know all that had passed, but not too young to fear lest she were dead, and had passed to some world not heaven. Yet the dream was not wholly evil now. Though her companion did not speak, she knew that he was a friend. When the castle was high above, and the great woods thronged all around, she grew bold enough for a question.

"Who are you?"

The hermit did not reply. In his heart he was repeating an awful warning,"Fear the Tempter now, Jerome; you lead by your hand—a woman!"

"Who are you?" repeated the little maid;"for I think you are surely God, since God looks like a tall and noble man with a long white beard, and all the wicked like Baron Ulrich haste to obey him."

"Do not blaspheme," commanded Jerome, swift as an arrow, almost casting off her hand;"I am the most sinful creature under heaven."

"Then you are the Devil. I have heard the Abbess call him 'The Old Man,' too, yet I think Baron Ulrich would never fear the Devil."

"Hush, daughter!" ordered the hermit, groaning gently at the manifold tribulations he saw awaiting;"my name is Jerome of the Dragon's Dale. Your poor mind wanders after all the griefs of the day. Now how were you christened?"

"Agnes; and my father is Graf Ludwig of the Harz."

"Agnes—that is a good name for a maid. I knew an Agnes once—"

"Your own child?"

"She was—" but the words seemed to come almost as a sob; and with instinctive delicacy the girl feared to press her guide with questions.

In silence they went down into the very deeps of the forest. Agnes scarcely saw the glimmerings of moonlight under the matted trees. She heard the noise of hidden beasts, the whirl of hidden waters. Then her guide felt the hand drag heavy in his own, and he bent over her.

"What is it? Why do you draw back?"

"Pixies are here. I am afraid."

"There are no pixies here; yet if there were, they are not for dread. A Christian maid need only fear the wrath of sinful men. So say 'Our Father' and be brave. Yet you grow weary?"

"Yes."

The strong frame bowed. The hermit lifted his prisoner in his mighty arms. How light the form! Something that sent a thrill all through him touched on his cheek,—the soft hair of a maid. His stride grew longer. Presently on his shoulder, close to his ear, was a sound. He halted at the break in the trees, where spread the moonlight. No room for doubt; utterly worn, even whilst he bore her, Agnes was in the child's safe refuge,—sleep. As Jerome moved, he also deemed himself a dreamer. He, Jerome of the Dragon's Dale, was taking to his hut a woman! What matter if that temptress was a child, robed in white innocency and help-lessness? She was not less the daughter of Eve by whom our fathers fell. Bear her to Witch Martha? But that unholy woman's den was two good leagues away, and then what right had he to put this Agnes's soul in eternal jeopardy by casting her into company with that familiar of Satan? Jerome felt the warm breath and the soft hair, and saw in the black shadows the form that trusted him.

"She imagined you were God!" Then he said in his heart that this was one of Christ's little ones, and that he must be strong in temptation. By the time he had reached the Dragon's Dale the burden in his arms had grown heavy. Unhesitant he threaded the familiar path, and mounted the slope. Before the hut still glowed a few red embers. He took the maid inside, and laid her on the furze bed. She folded her hands, sighed prettily, but did not waken. Jerome stole from the hut, then fell on his knees to pray. "O Lord God, why hast Thou appointed that I cannot beat back memory! It all awakes! Ah! save me from new temptation. I cannot bear after so long that I should fail, and pawn once more my soul and the soul of Sigismund, my son!"

CHAPTER IV
THE DOVE AT THE DRAGON'S DALE

WHEN Maid Agnes passed from dreams to the first slow waking, she did not open her eyes. Beneath her head was something soft and fragrant,—balmy furze and the sweet boughs of pine. Outside and all about was a crooning, witching sound,—the great pines and beeches talking. Memory throbbed back; but memory without a pang. Journey, fray, blood and slaughter, the Wartburg and its godless crew, all seemed an hundred years away. She could look back on them calmly, gladly, as do the saints on high upon the distant pains of the little, fading earth. Where was she? She did not know; still less did she care. Outside the pines kept at their sighing and talking. She could almost catch the words. Far, far away, as from a distant world, pealed out a bell,—the matin-bell of Eisenach; she stirred and opened her eyes. The little hut was dark, but athwart the doorway streamed a golden sunbeam enticing her. Short was the toilet; she was outside the hut. The great trees were bending overhead. Through the rifts in the boughs peered down the blue of clearest heaven. No human form was in sight, but before the hut a noble flame crackled; trees before, behind, to right, to left. But all was peace, and every tree seemed as a friend. Now her ears caught the noise of rushing water. A step down the slope brought her to a rill, where leaped a streamlet clear and cold from its fountain. She bathed hands and face in the little pool, and saw the buttercups drifting as tiny boats across the water. In the twinkling mirror she saw her own softly moulded face, and bound back the flying gold-brown hair. Then at last she knew she was hungry, even in heaven, and looked about her.

Feet were crunching the dead leaves of the forest. Out of the coppice came a man,—her deliverer of the night before. She ran to him with beaming face, and held out her hands.

"Oh! It is you who saved me from Baron Ulrich; and I know now who you are. My wits were straying last night, but to-day it is all plain! We are near Eisenach, and you are Saint Jerome of the Dragon's Dale."

"Who declared that?" and poor Jerome was wondering whether to open his arms and welcome the vision into them, or to flee as from the embrace of Satan arrayed like an angel of light.

"The Abbess at Bamberg; and My Lord the Prince Bishop has written concerning you to Rome, to the Holy Father. Ah! saint you must be, that Baron Ulrich should thus dread you! I remember all now!"

Jerome did not answer. So his fame had spread to Rome! Well that Witch Martha had not told all this, or his visit to the Wartburg would have cost yet sorer mental wrestlings than it surely did! Agnes came very close to him, and still with both arms wide.

"Ah! my father Graf Ludwig is a strong, rich man, and will reward you,—but what do I say! Are you not a saint, and what would be gold or lands or vassals, when the dear God is giving you a great fief up in heaven! Yet I must do something."

They stood eyeing one another—those twain—like two champions in the lists. Then the maid, reckless through youth and love, caused Jerome to be tempted of the Devil.

"Oh! it will not be so very wrong! even if angels come each night to kiss you! I must kiss you too."

And so she did, putting her arms about him, and kissing his shaggy lips, and saying all the cooing tender things which spring from the heart of a child. Jerome did not thrust her back. He told himself that here was a last test sent from heaven, to see if he could endure the kiss of a maid, and never yearn for worldly joys thrust by. But he did not return the kiss, and she added, a little grieved:

"You are not angry with me?"

"No, daughter, no; but are you not hungry?"

"That I am."

Jerome took from the wicker basket which he bore six speckled trout, his morning booty, cleaned dexterously, and soon, spitted on twigs, they hung above the fire. An instant later Harun burst through the thicket, in his mouth a partridge. But Agnes gave a little shriek, and made to fly.

"A wolf!"

Jerome assured her with a nod.

"He never harms."

"But wolves are evil beasts;" and Agnes still shrank, as Harun laid his trophy at his master's feet.

"The only evil beasts are men."

"I forget that he is a saint," said Agnes, under breath,"and all things of the forest must obey him."

So the partridge broiled beside the trout, whilst Harun dutifully waited for the bones. Jerome brought forth bread and cheese,—the simplest meal in Agnes's life. What would my Lady Abbess at Bamberg think to have a beech leaf in her lap, in lieu of a fair white napkin from Flanders? But was it hunger which made all taste so good, or was it that a real saint had asked God's blessing?

After the feast was over, Harun shambled away into the wood, and Agnes looked at the hermit, questioning.

"What am I to do?"

"Go where you will; follow down the stream, but stop when you come to the close gorge of the Dragon's Dale. If you never quit the brook, you can never get lost. When you are weary, come back."

So she kissed him once more, and clambered down the hillslope, whilst Jerome straightway took out the scourge as antidote for earthly imaginings.

But Agnes found all the groves and hills one kingdom of delight; for what bad sprites dared dwell so near a saint? Upon the boughs grave thrushes winked down at her; little green snakes shot in and out the grass. Once she pushed back a bush, and came face to face with two bright, gentle eyes,—a cow? what cow had ever horns like these? A snort, a stamping—away scampered the deer, and she heard him leaping through thicket on thicket. She followed the stream past tiny pool and waterfall till she halted at the mouth of the Dragon's Dale; for here she was sure the holy spell of the great saint ended, and gnomes and goblins ruled in that serpent-like ravine. So she turned back, with pleasures enough in the forest, until suddenly she came on a human being,—a quaint little woman, seated on a log, with two ravens croaking on her shoulders. The little woman (despite her round waist) dropped Agnes a very deep courtesy, called her"my gracious lady," and seemed as much a gentle-woman as the Abbess herself, notwith-standing strange costume and stranger resting-place.

"And are you a holy woman too?" asked Agnes, when the first edge was off her wonder;"for you are not at all like to Jerome?"

Here the little woman rocked with laughter till the woods reechoed, and a redbreast whirled out of a beech in fright.

"Who are you, then?"

"Call me Witch Martha."

Agnes began to grow pale about her lips; but the new friend assured her that hers was only"white magic," that she was as good a Christian as any in the Thuringerwald, and that all her elves and dwarfs were second cousins to the angels, only they could not live up in heaven because of a little swarthiness of their skins. Then Witch Martha drew Agnes down upon her log, and before long the brown head was in the little woman's lap, and soon Martha had heard all of Agnes's brief life-story,—how her mother had died when she was a baby, and how she had always lived at the great Abbey of Bamberg, under the special eye of the noble Abbess, who was the Prince Bishop's own sister. As for her father, Graf Ludwig, all Germany knew that he was a great prince in the North Country, rising every day in favour with the Landgraf of Thuringia, and with the new Emperor, Rudolf of Hapsburg, and with them trying to end the "stirrup law" of Ulrich and his kind. Agnes had never been far from the convent; she knew rather less of the world than Martha's winking ravens; she could embroider, sing, read a little Latin, and illuminate a missal. She had seen her father only twice. He was a grand, tall man, very fierce, but magnificent; something about him reminded her of Jerome the Saint. But he was no saint,—Our Lady pity him!—he was too fond of forays and tourneys, for that! Nevertheless, Agnes was very proud of him; and at Goslar—whither he had summoned her—no doubt she was to live in state like an Elector's daughter.

Witch Martha only nodded her wise head, seemed to ask few questions, really asked many, and found out all she wished to know.

"Has your father always lived in the North Country?"

Agnes thought not. The nuns at Bamberg had never told her much about his early life, because, forsooth, they did not know themselves. But old Sister Barbara had once said that the Graf had surely been in Italy and even in the Holy Land, and Sister Elizabeth, the faultfinder of the nunnery, had added that much travel amongst the paynims had surely brought him into perilous disregard for his soul. But the Abbess had ordered "silence, and no chattering of things whereof few save the Recording Angel knew certainly."

Then Agnes had her own question. Who was Jerome? Had he always dwelt by the Dragon's Dale? Was he not of all men very holy?

Witch Martha answered with all seeming candour that there was no man from Pomerania to Swabia more loved of God than he, so that Saint Gabriel had lately assured Saint

Raphael how he had heard our Father say that when Jerome went to heaven he was to be His archchancellor, just as the Bishop of Koln was to Kaiser Rudolf. Nevertheless Jerome had only been by the Dragon's Dale these seven years, but since coming he had charmed the wolves, the foxes, and the red deer so that they all served him like so many varlets.

"Yet who is he?" would ask Agnes;"was he never young? For I can never think how he looked when once a child, as I can think of you, Witch Martha."

The little woman seemed to shiver and to sigh, as if she, too, had a war with memory, but answered:—

"Only Heaven knows his age, and Heaven will not tell! Yet I think this,—that once he was a man of strong deeds and of blood, like Graf Ludwig; that he has been in many distant lands, for he speaks the paynim tongue even better than the German. And I think that once he had a son."

"A son? A little lad?"

"No; for his son had grown to be a tall knight, and though Jerome keeps all hid, I think that father and son had a bitter quarrel,—they parted in anger, and soon after the son died, still cursed of his father. Therefore Jerome has God's anger weighing upon him heavily, and he fears for his son's salvation."

"And on this account did Jerome turn saint?"

"I think so."

Agnes sighed and looked wise."It must be hard to learn to be a saint; yet now he must enjoy it. Still, I have not seen him smile. Surely they must smile up in heaven. Saint Peter and Saint Paul, Saint Lorenz and Saint Sebastian,—Sister Rosala said that because they had toil and martyrdom on earth, they never lacked good wine and merry minne-lays in their great castles in the Golden City."

"No doubt she is right," quoth Martha, laughing now, though strangely enough her laugh seemed close to tears;"but our Saint of the Dragon's Dale is not raised to heaven yet."

CHAPTER V
JEROME IS TEMPTED OF THE DEVIL

WHEN Agnes came again to the hut, she saw no sign of Jerome. But Harun was there, and for a moment maid and wolf looked on one another, questioning; each meditating whether to make friends, or to fly incontinently into the forest. Agnes had learned by heart Sister Rosala's tale of the big demon Elemauzer, who liked nothing better than to scamper over the world in the form of a tawny wolf, to snap up juicy girls; while Harun's knowledge of human kind was summed up in Jerome, Witch Martha, and a certain poacher who twice had nearly winged him with an arrow. But there seemed nothing demoniacal in Harun, and nothing dangerous in Agnes. Therefore, Harun drew near very timidly, wagged his tail, let his red tongue hang out and puffed in friendship, whilst Agnes still more timidly put a small hand betwixt his ears and stroked him. Then from armed truce sprang peace, from peace came comradeship; and before either knew it, Harun was drowsing on the greensward, sinking deeper and deeper into slumber, and Agnes's gold-brown head lay on his tawny shoulder. The great boughs far above never ceased their talking, and gossiped louder as the south wind, kind and warm, sung over the summer forest. The wood-thrushes whistled in and out; over Agnes's face great bumblebees buzzed closely, half wondering whether in her red lips there lurked no sip of honey. But she never heard their pragmatic droning, for Harun, sly protector, gave his tail a mighty slap which sent the bees away to less safe-guarded flowers. So noon sank down toward evening. The shadows of the pines were longer, longer. The breeze had sung itself to sleep, and all the woods grew still. Then through the fern-brake stirred Jerome, walking tenderly,—for he would not needlessly crush a dewy blossom,—and stood beside the silent pair.

Jerome had been over hill and dale to Witch Martha's dwelling with the laudable desire to acquaint that uncanny woman concerning the results of his mission to the Wartburg, and to bid her seek out some one who could communicate with Graf Ludwig and take the child away. He was sorely tempted to deliver Agnes to Martha, and so rid himself of all temptation. Again he told himself it was no safe thing to trust a little maid to one who might sell her protégé's soul to Devil Baalberith for two Bremen shillings. Martha, however, for her own reasons had remained abroad, and Jerome, when the sun sank, turned homeward—his charge could spare him no longer. Yet not altogether regretful. Something, some one, would be awaiting him at the hut. He would hear a voice,—not his own, not Harun's shrill bark, not the cry of the wood-bird. He would look into human eyes, he would feel a hand, he would—"*Ne nos inducas in tentationem,*" prayed

Jerome;"plain, plain it is, Lord, Thou hast given me over to Satan, even as Thou didst Thy servant Job, to see if I can endure all and stand." First he looked in the hut, and was troubled at finding no form upon the furze bed; then beside the tall tree he saw the sleepers, and almost ere he knew it his lips were twitching in a smile,—*O maximum peccatum! O gaudium impium!* Joy, not at the contemplation of the beatific vision, but at sight of a noxious beast and of a mortal maid! Nevertheless, as he stood over them, these were the words which seemed sounding.

"And the sucking child shall play on the hole of the asp, and the weaned child shall put his hand on the cockatrice's den; they shall not hurt nor destroy in all my holy mountain?'

But Jerome only told himself that Satan could wrest Scripture as fairly as an angel; then fortified against temptation he touched Agnes.

"Awake!"

The heavy eyes opened, stared around.

"Ah! but the shadows are long! It grows dark," said she all wondering, whilst Harun rose and shook his coat free of the pine-needles.

"Yes, you must have slept soundly. It is time to eat;" and Jerome busied himself about the supper,—more trout, bread, cheese, and the remnants of the partridge. He studiously refrained from glances at Agnes, and never spoke save as he must. When the meal ended, Agnes held her pretty head first this way, then that, and followed with a statement.

"I met a woman by the brook."

"A woman? of what kind?"

"A fat little woman all in black, with two big blacker

ravens."

Jerome frowned."Then you have met Witch Martha. She has commerce with the Father of Lies; shun her carefully or you can never go to heaven."

"Oh, but she did nothing wicked. Her speech had far more about Our Lady and the Blessed Saints in it than you hear with the sisters at Bamberg."

"Her tongue may have a jargon of piety, but her soul is given to Satan."

Agnes sighed. Jerome was a saint, and he ought to know. Yet it was perplexing to understand that so prepossessing a woman as Martha had stricken hands with the Devil. Presently Agnes began again.

"Holy Saint Jerome, why do you never smile?"

"Have I not told you I was no saint?" and he waxed almost angry.

"Witch Martha and My Lady Abbess say that you are, and I believe they, not you, are right."

There bubbled to Jerome's lips an imprecation against those two women which might have seemed worthy of Baron Ulrich's self. Jerome checked it just in time."At least," he comforted himself,"the arising of such blasphemies in my heart proves that I am still a naked sinner."

"Maid Agnes," said he, severely,"Witch Martha and the Abbess prattle folly. I am a very wicked man."

"Is it for that cause you will not smile?"

"Yes;" but he knew she was incredulous.

"Not even if I weave these purple asters and buttercups in a wreath, and set it on your head?"

He did not answer. Conscience told that he ought to rebuke her for tempting him from holy meditations. Why disobey the dictate? Yet he did. She made the wreath.

He felt the little flowers upon his hair. He felt the touch of her soft hands upon his cheek; and her eyes looked straight into his.

"Smile!" she commanded, as she might address Harun;"do you hear me, smile!"

And Jerome—that saint adored through wide Thuringia—obeyed her. He smiled; he almost laughed; but—praised be Saint Simeon—grace was given just to shun that!

Once more the silvery bell in distant Eisenach knelled across the trees, calling to vespers. They knelt down to pray. Jerome had even forgotten to doff the flower crown. The maid prayed in loud whisper,—to Our Lady, to Agnes of Rome her patron saint,—then added something more softly, but he could hear it,"Holy Saint Jerome of the Dragon's Dale, pray for me."

Why did he not rebuke her with the thunders of Sinai? Why did his own prayer halt? Had Witch Martha taught the maid some guilty spell? Had the arch-fiend taken a young girl's shape to overcome this hardened anchorite? But Jerome was silent, and Agnes arose from her knees.

"How long can I stay here?" spoke she, before she went into the hut to lie down.

"I shall try to send at once for Graf Ludwig."

"Oh! he can know that I am safe; but it is lovely here! I do not want to go away. Harun, the brook, and the birds, and the talking trees, already I love them, but most of all,—*you*."

Then he let her kiss him good night. He did not return the kiss; nevertheless he groaned inwardly, knowing he was making progress in sin. True was Master Vergil's word,"*Facilis descensus Averni!*"

As he sat in the waning firelight, for the first time in many a month a profound loneliness had stolen over him. Harun had prowled away into the forest. Presently Jerome arose, cast a fresh branch on the fire, and stole into the hut."I must see if she is safe and warm."

Through the doorway crept a silver-sandalled moon-beam. It touched on something round and white,—the face of the little maid. All Jerome's veins seemed turned to fire, yet all that fire was ineffably sweet.

He knew the glow and ecstasy of the soul born into highest heaven. A power not sprung of self compelled him. He could not resist; he would not if he could. Bending across that face, he kissed it with his bearded lips. Once,—and the fire leaped into more exquisite heat; twice, thrice, four times,—but at the fourth his soul fell down from its high heaven, like Lucifer, son of the Morning. He rushed from the hut, his heart torn by demons, its fire a maddening pain.

"He, *he*—Jerome of the Dragon's Dale—had bestowed a kiss on a maid!"

* * *

Jerome had resolved not to sleep that night. He must battle back the fiends, as became a holy soldier. The terror lest he had fallen utterly; lest by this one lapse the credit laid up with God by years of austerity was forfeit,—this was omnipresent. He would have scourged himself, but the whip lay under the bed of the little maid, and now he was most certain that in approaching Agnes he approached a form of Satan. So he knelt and thought that he prayed; but his head was heavy. Thrice he shook the stupor off: but strive as he would, unholy dreams rose uppermost. Women were rising before him, foul and pure, hideous and beautiful. Was it the Blessed Virgin enringed by a host of glittering spirits who was beckoning, who was calling him? No; he knew her now,—it was the Norse King's daughter, the golden-haired Trolfreda, and the wind that hummed about blew not from the crystal river but from the blue breast of the wild North Sea. Again she was changed,—she was Ada of the Silver Belt, and he rode into Orleans at her palfrey's side, whilst bright tabarded heralds cried him the stoutest knight of the Loire; but his fairest glory was in the lady's eyes. Yet again the heralds wore crimson turbans, their faces were black, in their hands boomed paynim atabals. The church spires were spindling minarets. The air was sweet with the musky breath of desert sands. It was not Orleans, but Al-Cairo by the Nile. Obaëdah was leaning down from the swaying camel. He could see the gemmed bracelets twinkling upon her smooth brown arms, the gold upon her raven hair, the rosy lips which parted in the snaring smile. And then back to the tourney at Naples: Kaiser Frederick, crowds, plaudits, crowns,—and Mathilde,—the walk with Mathilde by the sea.

He woke from the vision with a scream of mortal pain. The black woods rang; a frightened bird whirred from her nest. Jerome never knew it. He was in cold sweat from foot to crown, and trembling. So far from praying he had given place to sinful lusts. All the passions of the old life surged back in one fierce wave. The repression of years had gone for nothing. His sins stared him tenfold blacker than the night. Again on his knees he prayed out loudly:—

"O Lord Jesus Christ, if Thou hast any mercy, take far from me this maid, or my soul and the soul of Sigismund my son are lost forever! Thou knowest how I am tempted past endurance. For surely Beelzebub, Sifter of Souls, has sent this child to bring back every ungodly wish and thought. Her power on me is grown so strong! Away with her, Lord! in Thy Blessed Mother's name,—away with her! or I know not what to do!"

So he prayed long and loud, never heeding whether any ears save those of the wood-birds heard him. He never recked a single, soft, sobbing cry, and the noise of feet receding in the forest. Then came sleep,—as wicked as before. He sank away with a godless song of Walter von der Vogelweide trolling in his ear,—a minne-song in praise of love and laughter in springtime. When he awoke, lo! the ruddy dawn was tinting the greensward. The fire was dead. By instinct he ran to the hut. Empty. He called the girl.

"Agnes! Agnes! Where?"

No answer came. The shouts died down the avenues of trees. He hunted near. He hunted far. The maid had vanished in the night. He should have thanked our Lord his prayer was so swiftly granted. He did nothing of the kind. He was almost cursing Heaven for making his petition good. With eyes aflame, with heart nigh leaping in his throat, he ran toward the Dragon's Dale. He must find the maid,—yes, though to find her he bartered his own soul and his son's.

CHAPTER VI
THE HERALD OF THE KAISER

THE Wartburg was in commotion; men ran this way and
that through barbican and bailey. Michael the Breaker
looked to see if the portcullis was ready to drop at a
hatchet stroke. Franz of the Ram's Pate brandished a
battle-axe of three stone, and Priest Clement clapped on
a helmet.

A herald had come to the Wartburg. He wore the Imperial arms, the double eagle of the Hapsburgs upon his
orange surcoat. He reined his white mule at the gate of the
Vorburg, and wound a long blast upon his silver horn.
Then his roaring summons roused all the castle."Ho!
Ulrich of Eisenach! come forth, come forth and listen to the
summons of your liege lord and emperor!"

But Ulrich safe in the inner Hofburg swore a great oath
by Saint Jacobus that the herald might bawl until the
bastion cracked before he stirred to hear him; and the
herald, having waited duly and gotten only curses through
the loophole, completed his proclamation.

"In the Name of the Blessed Trinity, Amen!

"I, Rudolf, Crowned of God, Emperor of the Romans, Graf of Hapsburg, and Freiherr of Argau, to Ulrich of Eisenach, and all who follow him,—greeting:—

"I do summon you to appear before my assize at Goslar, on the third Monday hereafter following, to answer by what warrant you do hold this castle of the Wartburg to the detriment of its lawful master, our well-beloved cousin the Landgraf of Thuringia; and by what warrant you have halted, robbed, and slain divers of our loving subjects upon our highways, in violation of our Imperial peace.

"And especially we command you, under pain of our most condign displeasure, to deliver instantly to this our herald the noble lady, Agnes, daughter of our trusty vassal Graf Ludwig of the Harz, whom you do detain in most unlawful custody.

"And each and all of you who shall defy these our commands, we declare under our Imperial Ban, and as such our loyal subjects are commanded to apprehend or extirpate. Also by the special authorization of the holy Apostolic Inquisitor, the Archbishop of Mainz, we declare all contemners of our decrees excommunicated from the sacraments of Holy Church.

"God save Kaiser Rudolf!"

So cried the herald; and when no intention was manifested of delivering up the Lady Agnes to him, he blew another great blast, and rode down the steep to leave Baron Ulrich and his merry men clear at their wits' last end.

No one could doubt that the extermination of Maid Agnes's escort had been incomplete. Some one had escaped and told Graf Ludwig. The lion was unchained in very deed! In the great feasting hall the council met, but there was no wassail now. Ulrich's scarred face was black with rage and dread. Priest Clement had nearly forgotten his scraps of Latin. The situation was plain enough. All through the wild and wicked years following the death of Frederick the Second, Thuringia had belonged to the bandit barons who had watched the roads and ruled by"fist-law." The power of the Landgraf had sunk to a shadow, and Ulrich and his crew had held the Wartburg for a decade. But there was a new kaiser now who had begun to end the merry dance of devils. Rumours blew north,—how in Swabia Kaiser Rudolf had beaten down castles and hanged many a reckless"ritter" on the pine tree facing his own smoking keep. And Graf Ludwig, the Imperial Vicar, had come to Thuringia with a goodly force to do the very same deeds; therefore My Lord Ulrich had his food for thought.

"How many men will the Graf bring?" he was asking.

"I have heard said," quoth Michael, sullenly,"he has more than two thousand, with battering mangonels, likewise a band of English longbowmen who came with Duke Richard of Cornwall and remained. No crossbows can match their archery."

"And we have an hundred and twenty dogs at most, and the Wartburg, though strong, has a vast circuit to defend. If cleared of this plight, I vow Saint Moritz of Coburg a chalice of heavy gold! Is that overdear for the worthy saint's aid—eh! Clement?"

Ulrich leered at the priest, and the holy man twisted his nose, while meditating. "A pious vow, noble Baron, a very pious vow! Nevertheless,—humph!—what did you say? How long did you think we could make good the castle?"

"Two days at most," snarled Michael, crossly.

"Two days, and then to heaven!" ran on Clement;"will the ladder be axe, sword, or rope? Ah! *Gratias Deo,*—a thought!"

"What?"

"That the wench Agnes is still with the hermit. It is wrong to outrage a saint *sed necessitas non habet legem;* and we can also add a trifle to the weight of the chalice. In brief, seize her from the hermit, hold her hostage; and when the Graf comes, force him to promise us at least our lives in exchange for her safety."

"The saint will rage," objected Michael.

"If your wisdom knows a better salve against the little pains of hanging, I am listening," laughed Clement, dryly. Whereat Ulrich leaped up with a jangle of armour.

"Priest Clement has the only sense. Be Jerome saint or devil, he must not keep the maid. Out, every man and lad; arm heavily, and away to the Dragon's Dale!"

Therefore it befell that an hour later, just as the sun was scattering the last mists of the morning, the Baron led out his force,—an hundred odd of as hardened sinners as ever put on harness. Nevertheless it took all his oaths, and the well-grounded fears of a swift voyage to a nether country, to make the file advance when they began to enter the charmed region around the Dragon's Dale.

When they reached the cross where burgomaster Gottfred had been stricken, even Michael the Breaker wished to halt and pray. Ulrich and Clement walked behind with their lances to prod on the laggards. They reached the mouth of the Dragon's Dale, and every man stood irresolute, nigh convinced that the first wight inside the ravine would be frozen into a black stone in a twinkling. Yet as they scuffled and shrank, lo! straight out from the wall of rock came running the saint himself, his white hair spread like a lion's mane, wild fire in his eyes, his hands upraised now in prayer, now in cursings.

"In the name of the Lord Christ,—where? where?"

"Where, what?" demanded Ulrich, trembling, but not so much as before; there was nothing awesome in the hermit now.

"The maid! Maid Agnes, the Graf's daughter? She has vanished. You have stolen her. Oh! may the curse of God light swift on you!"

He was nigh crazed, and a mere madman was not very terrifying. So they plucked up courage, and stood their ground.

"Hark you, greybeard," warned the Baron, roughly;"it is for the wench we are come ourselves. Do you think we would rout you out of your accursed den without fair cause? The maid we will have, or by the Trinity,—" he broke off, the threat unfinished, and glared on the hermit, who appeared utterly unstrung. For an instant he seemed only the shambling dotard.

"Gone! gone," he moaned abjectly."I can find her nowhere. If you fiends do not possess her, she has perished amongst the cruel beasts."

The Baron was brave now, and advanced boldly.

"Here, Michael,—a cord; pinion this babbler. We'll hale him to the Wartburg, and then if the wench is not found, there'll be tortures to wring out of him where he is hiding her. Forward, lads; there's nothing dreadful."

He snatched Jerome by the arm. Men looked to see a bolt crash down from heaven. None came. Jerome submitted like a lamb. Michael and Clement were at least brave enough to stand at either side as guards. Ulrich led thirty of his boldest down the Dragon's Dale, crossbow strung, swords bare,—half disappointed they did not meet a fire-breathing goblin. They found the little hut empty; they searched about the tree—only birds and dragon-flies. Maid Agnes was nowhere. Ulrich returning promised Jerome smart torture if the girl was not found. Jerome gave back not a word. So at last the Baron started again for the Wartburg with his prisoner, ordering the men to scatter through the greenwood, by fives and tens, and to scour knoll and dale for seven leagues about. Have the hostage they must, though they sought all night for her!

Once at the castle Ulrich ordered forth the bloodhounds. The pack went baying down the valley, the halloos of the hunt sounded far and wide in the forest; but when the *lanzknechts* dispersed in little bands, they knew too well the paling dread of pixies to pry over deeply into the secrets of the wood. The hounds ran down all scents—but vainly. Priest Clement swore that the Brown Dwarfs had stolen the queen down to their underworld."Where, alas for her poor soul, since they were pagans all!" he added as became a holy cleric. The chase wandered far from the Wartburg. Presently Ulrich, disheartened, angry, turned back to the castle, with Clement and Michael, leaving the rest to carry on the hunt. Saint or no saint, he intended to test his prisoner by torture to see if he were hiding Agnes by some art-magic. It would be an impious deed,—Ulrich knew it,—but better impiety, than the falling into Graf Ludwig's iron clutches!

The Wartburg was nigh empty when the Baron reentered. In the courts some of the slattern women had lit huge bonfires, which roared up to the deepening sky, making turret and rampart frown down grimly. Franz, who had played castellan in his lord's absence, reported the captive safe in the lower dungeon. The Baron cursed that no one had advised him to shoot down the herald, and so win extra time to prepare to face attack; but there was only one thing to do now. Leaving Franz and a bare dozen of men-at-arms to patrol the battlement, he summoned Priest Clement and Michael to fetch him divers instruments; then with them hastened down into the bowels of the great Wartburg rock.

All that stone and steel could do to secure Jerome had been done. He was in a cell whither no sun had crawled since the building of the Wartburg; but the hermit had recovered his dignity. He faced the three men of blood with a cold, stern stare, which stole away half their courage.

"Where is the maid?" demanded Ulrich, trying to set bravado up for valour.

"God knoweth, and in His wisdom keeps her hid, except you have already possessed yourselves of her, and seek this occasion against me."

Ulrich ostentatiously produced a mallet, and many little oaken wedges, while Clement raised the smoking torch. Then the Baron's tone grew threatening.

"Hear you, old man! be you saint or devil, we will have the maid. Whether angel or gnome has hidden her, and where, you know; and by Saint Moritz"—Ulrich felt safe invoking that martyr, in view of his vow,—"out with her hiding-place or try these pretty toys! Behold!"

The anchorite shrugged his shoulders with undisguised contempt.

"Ulrich of Eisenach," spoke he, sternly, "I answer you on the word of a Christian man, though a sinner, that I know not where the maid is. Doubtless it has pleased God to bring this thing to pass that you may rush headlong in your sins and dash to eternal perdition. As for these oaken splints, which you weakly design to drive betwixt my nails and fingers,—bethink you if a man like me, who has endured the worst gehennas of the paynim will flinch before your petty torments? Or what will they profit you, save to heat sevenfold the fires now lit for you in hell?"

Michael had been stripping back the sheepskin from the prisoner's shoulder. Then, as the light flickered over it, leaped back in horror.

"Holy Mother! His back,—all marked with scarce-healed scars!"

"Amen!" quoth Jerome, grimly; "those and all other tortures are too gentle for my sins. Yet, if I would glory after the flesh, I can make boast that all your tortures, Ulrich of the Wartburg, will be to me as nothing."

"He is right," groaned the Breaker, all his terrors springing up anew; "we are outraging God's saint. The demons will boil us forever!"

"Silence, fool," commanded Ulrich, grown desperate; "pass me yonder mallet, and hold fast his wrist. We will sound the depth of this loud boasting. Now and for the last time, babbler! Where hide you Agnes the maid?"

Jerome vouchsafed no reply. Ulrich was clutching the

mallet and sliver when Franz-of-the-Ram's-Pate burst into the prison. Even in the gloom his face shone white as a ghost's.

"Up, for the love of Christ! Horses and men are all about! The Wartburg is surrounded."

Whereat the three raced up from that dungeon, never waiting for the door to clash.

CHAPTER VII
FRITZ THE MASTERLESS

NOW when Agnes awoke from her sleep, when she heard Jerome at his prayer, when she heard him call to God to remove his temptress,—sent to vex him by Beelzebub, catcher of souls,—then a surge of sorrow, deeper than she had ever known before, had swept over her heart. She had cried once and softly; she had risen from her furze-bed, and reckless of everything had stolen away into the forest. Only one thing she knew,—the great saint hated her! He believed Satan had thrust her upon him. She was too sinful to bear company with this holy man, and must flee away, far away! All her heinous crimes rose up to stare her in the face, the thirty Aves her confessor had enjoined upon her, and which she had forgotten to say, the five spice-cakes which she had filched from My Lady Abbess's cupboard, and which she had never confessed at all,—these and more foul deeds weighed down her soul. The all-wise saint had beheld its vile-ness, and called to God to deliver her to her just possessor, Satan.

When she knew aught else the great black woods were

everywhere. There was only a flickering will-o'-the-wisp light here—there amongst the numberless trees. She dared not pray. Once she screamed, but the cry was dried up in her throat. In her blind anguish she wandered aimlessly through thorn and thicket, brier and brake. How many times she all but tripped into some ravine, or dashed on jagged rocks the angels in mercy hid, for Saint Azrael surely guided her wild feet then, though she thought the demons after her. At last spent with fatigue she sank upon a moss bank. An older person would have tossed and moaned till dawn; happier she—once more her eyes grew heavy. Fear and anguish vanished. She could sleep.

When Agnes this time woke it was with a start and with groaning. Trees, everywhere trees. The dawn was still young. The light was red. She was lonely, thirsty, hungry. There came a rambling rustle from the dead leaves near at hand. Hope leaped up that it was Harun, but only a tawny fox spread his proud brush and vanished, scampering at first sight of her. In these deepest glades of the beeches not a bird was carolling morning.

"Jerome! Holy Saint Jerome! I am wicked, but have pity. I am afraid of the great woods! Oh, in mercy lead me back!" Her shrill cry went out in mocking echoes from an unseen dell. Not a thrush called in answer. She sank into frightened silence. After long waiting she gathered courage to summon Witch Martha, but that good woman never came. At last Agnes, made calm by desperation, took counsel.

"I cannot stay here. I have nothing to eat. And I dare not die of hunger, for if I die, where is the priest to anoint me with the oil, and absolve my fearful sins? So I can never go to heaven. The woods cannot reach forever. No matter which way I go, sooner or later, I must come to some house of Christian folk who will pity me. Only I must walk a straight line and never turn back."

At least walking was easier than still agony; and she thrust boldly in among the trees. Before long she could quench her thirst in a tiny brook which sang along through hazel thickets. Then presently her heart gave a big throb. She was upon a path, weed-grown, leaf-strewn, yet a path, blazed through the forest. Surely it led to men, but whether a turn to right or left would reach a refuge soonest, Maid Agnes did not know. Therefore she made bold, despite her wickedness, to say a little prayer to Our Lady, asking her to guide the choice, shut her own eyes, and on one foot whirled around six times; then when she looked again, followed the way which lay straight before her. She might have walked the tenth of a league before a clearing burst into view,—walls, fruit trees, a garden, and an orchard, but everywhere silence and desolation. Here was the blackened foundation of a house and of two large barns, charred and rotting timbers, grass growing in the chinks of the mortar. The dwelling had been burned these two years. Yet Agnes was vastly comforted. The cherry trees of the orchard were heavy with round red fruit. A beam had fallen so that she could reach to a lower bough and pluck her fill. From the wild garden a linnet rose, interrupted in her feast of strawberries. Agnes had these too. The roses were climbing up the blackened wall, and the huge bees hung over them. Gorgeous butterflies spread their sails, and were wafted to and fro. But for the absolute solitude and the compelling fear, Agnes would have found this ruin the outer door to paradise. The sun had risen clear and warm, and the wood was giving forth the fragrant smell of green things growing. She ate cherries and strawberries until hunger was banished; then at last came time to consider"what next?" For no human help seemed here.

She was sitting upon the beam, her head on two small hands, when a man's shout startled her like a thunderclap.

"Heigh-ho! Have we here a Queen of the Pixies?"

Agnes looked up, and behold a man stood by, but not a steel-capped *lanzknecht* of Ulrich as first fears told her. The stranger was a short, wiry man, very black, with a huge mustache, a beard cut to a most singular little peak. He was all dressed in untanned doeskin; a hunting-bag slung on his shoulder; in his belt gleamed twenty steel-tipped bolts; in his hand was a crossbow. He did not look at all fierce, and Agnes put on dignity.

"I am the daughter of Graf Ludwig of the Hare, and am lost in the forest. Place me in safety, and my father will reward you."

"Graf Ludwig! By Saint Lorenz!" The little man made the greenwood ring with laughter."I have distinguished company on my domain. And how came you to get lost?"

But alas! the story which Maid Agnes told her new friend was too wandering to seem to have overmuch truth in it,—Saint Jerome, the Abbess, and Baron Ulrich, all jumbled hopelessly together. The fellow was only certain that a very rare bird had fluttered by a miracle into his net, and he was bound not to lose such gay feathers. So he merely took her by the hand, saying:—

"Come with me; you will soon be safe and happy."

"Where are we going?"

"To my cave; it is snug enough for a princess."

"A cave,—not a house? Who are you?"

"My best name is Fritz the Masterless. First I was a peasant and followed a stupid plough, then I was a swineherd, then a man-at-arms, then a *lanzknecht* and watched the roads, but all my band was cut to pieces, saving I, so I am now a poacher and a forest rover, and last of all, when the saints will, I shall be a gallows-bird, with a hemp collar and a dance on nothing, but *mm! zum!*—till then it is a merry life under the greenwood, a-following the deer." Agnes hung back.

"You are an evil man," she said soberly;"I will not go with you."

"And be left to wander under the trees, with never a house within these three leagues. Hoch! No, little lady; there is nothing gained by that. Come you do, will you, nill you."

The clasp on her hand tightened. Agnes knew resistance was vain. She followed silently, but her lips twitched. Oh! if she had been only sinless enough to dwell with holy Jerome.

* * *

In the deeps of the woodland Fritz the Masterless had his hold,—half cave, half hut, under the towering Rothenstein,—a cliff of gnarled red rock. Here Gerda, his strong-armed, swarthy wife, came to him, with Wolf his eldest, a sinewy lad of fourteen who could run like a rabbit, and also the pair of younger girls, coarse, tow-headed wights, who resembled Maid Agnes as two mongrels do a Castilian spaniel. They surveyed the father's booty with rude, gaping eyes, and Gerda sought greedily to see if the stranger wore no precious ring or jewelled crucifix; but

Priest Clement had done that work too well, and she was disappointed. However, there was no doubting the value of Fritz's catch. Such white skin and hands! Such silken hair and dainty face! She might be the Kaiser's own daughter; and her dress, if sadly torn, was of very silk from the great Cham's own country!

Agnes bore all more steadfastly than one might dream. There was a *ritter's* red blood in her veins if she had been reared in the Bamberg convent. She protested stoutly that she was Graf Ludwig's child, until Dame Gerda began to believe there was some fire behind so much smoke. So leaving Agnes to Wolf and the girls, she drew Fritz beyond earshot.

"She does not lie. She is the Graf's own child. And Ulrich of the Wartburg is back of her plight, I am bound."

"Humph!" commented Fritz; "it is a parlous thing to have dealings with the Graf, or with Ulrich either. Ulrich will hang me for taking his deer; the Graf for watching the roads. I am none too anxious for a voyage to purgatory that I desire to send a message to Ludwig, 'I have found your daughter.' He will come with five hundred men in lieu of ransom, and my best reward will be a long drop to the slip-noose."

Gerda considered wisely.

"Such white skin and hands! There is a fortune in her."

"Out with it then."

"Wolf shall go to Eisenach to Mordecai the Jew. He smuggles many a wench south to Italy, though the saints know what becomes of them then! He will give us round groschens for her."

Fritz frowned. His conscience troubled him, though only a little.

"If only Mordecai were not an unbeliever! It is wrong to deliver Christians into the clutch of infidels. I have heard he sells his women as far as to the Muslims."

But Gerda had only a hoarse laugh. "Pray for her soul if you will! One must live; and I will not see so much good silver glide out of my fingers vainly!"

Therefore her spouse reluctantly consented, and presently Wolf had his orders, and went away slyly northwards toward Eisenach.

Agnes was left in company with the girls. They gave her venison, and let her share the broth, which they all dipped with wooden spoons out of a great earthen pot. Her new acquaintances were decently respectful, although coarse enough in speech and life, to make their poor guest plagued indeed; but she needed little hinting that they were no friends, and that any attempt at flight would be hindered. The greenwood was still about Agnes; but it was only a hateful prison now, not an enchanted realm of cousins to the angels, as it was around the Dragon's Dale. Late in the afternoon Fritz came in with a long face.

"Men and hounds are out in the forest. They are beating up all the coverts. Ulrich has ordered a boar hunt. We must lie close."

So Agnes perforce, crouched with the rest, in a cavern up the rock-slope, until the clear hunting-horns died away in the distance, and Gerda began to thank the saints. As the gloaming fell, Wolf returned, and whispered to his mother that the Hebrew would set forth at dawn, and would be glad to haggle. Agnes did not hear the words, but she saw the glint in Dame Gerda's eye, and a cold shiver ran down her spine. The vagueness of her dread redoubled all the terrors, and hating all the rangers' loathsome company, Agnes wandered out a little way across the narrow meadow before the cave-hut. Wolf watched narrowly, but she did not try to flee away. Seated upon a stump she was watching the play of rosy light upon the scarred face of the Rothenstein,—when a whir of wings sounded, and whisk! something alighted upon her shoulder, then a voice, but not human:—

> "Ho, he! Never fear!
> I'm Satan! I'm here!"

"Zebek," cried Agnes,"oh, joy!"

The raven was welcome as a brother. Then the bird cocked his wicked head, and winked his sage eye, with which winking came a thought. To pluck the white lace from her wrist, to twine it round the raven's foot,—this was the deed of an instant.

"Back to Witch Martha; back! Fly fast, as you love me."

And Zebek,—wise beyond many a mortal, obeyed instantly, rising with one croak.

"Ho!" shouted Wolf, looking up;"a raven! Ill luck! Father, your crossbow!"

Fritz levelled in a trice;"whir" went the bolt, but it was growing dark. One feather fluttered to the grass; another croak from mid-air. Zebek was gone, winging straight west. Dame Gerda looked as black as the bird, when she came from the hut.

"A raven, ill luck," spoke she, and scolded Fritz and Wolf;"to slay a raven worse luck;but a vain bolt at a raven the worst luck of all. The bird will bear the grudge, and hatch us foulest weather."

CHAPTER VIII
GRAF LUDWIG

THE trap had snapped. Ulrich of Eisenach was in it. He had doubled the vow to Saint Moritz, but with no avail. In the last twilight the frighted watchers at the Wartburg peered from their turrets, and saw the dim masses of horse and footmen spreading themselves around the mountain,—hundreds, thousands. Graf Ludwig had been nearer, and in greater force than any *lanzknecht* dreamed. The Wartburg was ringed in by foes.

But this was not the worst. Ulrich's men were still beating up the forest, and the Graf had silently cut off their retreat. As they wandered home in sullen handfuls, cursing the bootless hunt, his sentries had nipped them, nearly all, taking prisoners after few struggles and fewer blows. Only two, slyer than the rest, had crept through the besiegers, and into the postern, with a tale which made Priest Clement's teeth chatter,—how Ludwig was at the gates with nigh three thousand men.

Ulrich had felt hard knocks from the Devil ere now, but this was the hardest. The Warburg was a very Emperor of castles,—provisioned and garrisoned by eight hundred, it could hold Kaiser Rudolf at bay. But inside the walls the Baron could barely count on twenty men fit to strike a blow, and the sluttish women were good for nought save screaming. Ulrich dropped the portcullis, placed a cata-pult to command the gate, and set boxes of arrows along the ramparts to insure ready ammunition; but how were a score to defend the long circuit of the battlement? The moat was almost dry. At dawn the Baron could kill a few attackers, but by the third hour after he knew well enough he would be voyaging toward heaven or elsewhere.

Desperate enough was every one in the Wartburg. As the night blackened, their mood blackened also. The sky was thickly clouded, starless, and moonless. A murky hot wind fanned from the south, dead and stifling,—"fit reminder," so Michael forced the jest,"of the breeze likely to blow in their next habitation." Priest Clement, who stood beside him on the gate tower, trembled all over at the impious levity.

"Do you not fear God? Are you so anxious for torment?"

"Humph!" grumbled the Breaker;"as much as you, holy Father. But I would have small respect for God if He were to forgive you or me now. We have made our bargain with Satan as do all fools, 'for a short life and a merry one,' and none should whine like a puppy if the landlord demands the 'drink-penny' at last.'

"You mean our souls?" moaned the priest.

"Very likely; ha! what is that?" and Michael levelled his crossbow into the dark. From the gloom below the gate came a deep voice.

"Ho! Ulrich of Eisenach; attend!"

"I am listening," bellowed the Baron from the tower;"who calls?"

"I,—Ludwig of the Harz; hear now and all your men! I command that you surrender the castle at dawn, that especially you deliver up to me, instantly and unharmed, my daughter, the Lady Agnes, likewise the holy hermit Jerome, whom your men say you hold prisoner. Your naked state is known to us. Escape is impossible. Surrender now, and I promise your lives and liberties, with no more penalty than the trifling striking off of your two thumbs, that you may never more draw bow, or swing longsword; if not—"

Ulrich's voice tossed back an angry answer."As for the Lady Agnes she is not with us. As for the hermit, when you storm the castle, we slay him. As for our thumbs they will swing our swords long enough to make your attack cost dear."

"Liar—do not say my daughter is not in your foul hold."

There was a ringing menace back of the word, which made even Ulrich quiver, and he turned to Franz.

"Go you and one other. Bring the hermit. Set him on the battlement. We will make him declare we have not the maid."

So whilst defiance passed they brought Jerome, told him how the land lay, and the Baron unsheathed a dagger.

"Speak him fair now, or take home this!" and he pricked with the point, but even in the dark they saw the hermit's grin of irony.

"Think you I am a child to fear the taste of steel? I say to you again," and Jerome's voice was almost proud,"I could teach even to demons like yourselves rare niceties in the arts of death and torture,—the hell-deeds of the Turks, of the Sicilians—"

"Silence," raged Ulrich;"here, set him upon the battlement. Now, my Lord Graf, hearken, as the hermit Jerome declares to you that we have not your daughter."

But Jerome only lifted his fettered hands, and called a terrible curse down on the Baron and his men.

"Smite! Smite and spare not! For the Lord has delivered these foes of His servants unto you. Root out His enemies. Let theirs be the fate of Dathan and Abiram, of Jezebel and Judas. Trust not their oaths, noble Graf, when they say they know nothing of your child. God knoweth the truth, but by their lies they would seek to deceive even Him and His Holy One!"

"Dash him down! Quench this madness!"

Thus cried Ulrich, but even Michael would not raise his sword.

"At least, let us not murder this saint *now!*" he resisted, and Ulrich blessed the darkness for hiding his own blenching skin. They haled Jerome back to his dungeon, and again through the dark came a summons."Hear then, men of the Wartburg. All, who by dawn shall come out to me, shall have their lives, saving always Ulrich of Eisenach, and Michael the Breaker, whose heads are forfeit to the Kaiser, and that unfrocked priest Clement, who is reserved for the merciful and paternal chastening of the most holy Inquisitor at Mainz."

But here Priest Clement began to groan terribly, fearing the rack and faggots even more than the subsequent strappadoes by Satan.

"And you, Hans Broadfoot, and you, Joachim the Smith,

except you surrender yourselves ere midnight, your brothers, whom I hold prisoners, have their feet wedged into split logs, and those logs most duly enkindled. Therefore, learn wisdom swiftly."

Whereupon two men-at-arms, who had been loudest and bravest for a fierce defence, became of a sudden thoughtful.

"And finally," wound up the Graf, "I do counsel that you kindle no torch nor fire upon the battlement; for I have placed Jack, Hodge, and Giles with twelve more picked English bowmen under your walls. Their eyes are like cats', and their cloth-yard shafts are the swiftest messengers to the Devil."

So with a dry laugh away went the chief into the dark, leaving the defenders as helpless as caged rats who see the farmer come to drown them.

There was nothing to be done. The long racks of lances in the great Waffensaal were mockery. No hands to wield them! The Wartburg was strong, but there was no donjon, separate from the outer hold, where a few desperate spirits could prolong resistance. Besides, succour was absolutely impossible. Before midnight, Hans and Joachim decided that they could not let their brothers be grilled just because they desired to have their throats cut at Ulrich's side in the morning. A little after midnight Michael killed a man who had tried to drop a rope from the battlement. Two hours after dawn, Ulrich, who had lain down, after leaving three men watching at the postern, returned and found only Franz.

"Where are the others?" asked the Baron.

"Deserted like the rest."

"And why not you?"

"Call me 'Ram's Pate 'an you will; I can still die with my master."

My Lord Baron had a choking in his throat. He gave Franz his mail-clad hand, then ordered him to summon Michael.

"All the rest have deserted, even the women," reported the Breaker, grimly. "In the Wartburg are you, Franz, Priest Clement, and your humble man-at-arms—not to mention the hermit down below."

"The joust ends," quoth My Lord. "The camp below is stirring; they attack us soon. Summon Clement. We must sound a parley with the saints, though he is an indifferent pursuivant."

In the wide, empty court they found the priest. His eyes were red, his gait unsteady. He had been heartening himself in the cellar, but when they told what they wanted he sobered quickly.

"Woe is me! All my sins flock home. It is I that need absolution."

"A priest is a priest, and at least we have none better," urged Michael, "therefore haste! Soon they will beat down the postern."

"Ay," lamented Clement, "'the validity of the sacrament depends not on the righteousness of the cleric, so runs the canon; but I am undone. None to absolve me, no masses, no indulgence! I am damned forever!"

"The hermit, the saint!" this from the slow Franz.

"The hermit! the saint!" so cried Clement; and they all ran down into the dungeon, dragged their prisoner up into the great hall, and tore off his fetters. He, expecting instant death, bowed his head in silent prayer, but did not try to escape. Then with the ruddy glare of dawn pouring through the eastern casement, those four wild men plumped on their knees before him.

"What do you wish?" said Jerome, opening his eyes.

"Oh, holy hermit, beloved of God," prayed Clement, catching at the anchorite's sheepskin,"absolve us, for we are nigh to death. We are sinful men, so hark to our confession."

Jerome frowned sternly."I am no priest," he shot back, nigh in wrath;"you who call yourself priest hear these men's confessions, and confess yourself to God. I am no intercessor for you."

"Not so," cried My Lord Baron, beginning to beat his breast;"you would not have us lost forever!"

"I am sinful like yourself. Refrain from sacrilege."

"Give attention, greybeard," admonished Michael, laying his battle-axe significantly beside him;"you have the ear of St. Peter and of St. Gabriel, and have it better than most bishops too. Bid them make us a smooth road to heaven, or it is the worse for you—by Our Lady of Lichtenfels—"

"Blaspheme not the Mother of God," thundered Jerome, as immovable as granite,"nor think by carnal threatenings to stir me."

"Confess first," advised Clement, sagely;"then we have but to wring *'absolvo'* out from his teeth, and we can sell our lives dear, fighting like the Christians that we are."

A rending crash without gave weight to his counsels.

"The postern yields," groaned Ulrich;"let us confess."

So all four beat their breasts, repeating their *mea culpas;*

then the Baron spoke first:—

"Hearken to my confession. I have sinned against God, His Mother, and the Holy Angels, inasmuch as I melted into a drinking-cup the golden crucifix which I took from the body of the Abbot of Nordhausen after that I had slain him."

And Michael the Breaker spoke:"Hear me. I also have sinned, inasmuch as last Ash Wednesday in my forgetfulness I ate the leg of a fowl at a farm-house we were pillaging."

And Franz of the Ram's Pate spoke:"Hear me. I also have sinned, inasmuch as I hunted a buck on the day of the last Communion, despising the holy sacrament."

And Priest Clement spoke:"Hear me. I also have sinned, inasmuch as forgetful of my sanctity as clerk, I did kiss the daughter of mine host of the 'Crown and Bells' the last Sunday that I was in Eisenach."

"And now," commanded Ulrich, roundly,"speak it out, the word *'absolvo.'*"

What strange thing played on Jerome's stern face? Was it the smile of the avenging angel or of the demon who sees his sinking prey? Louder the crash and wrack without. The Graf was almost in the Wartburg. Jerome's eyes seemed burning into all the four.

"Is this *all?*" demanded he, implacably."Have you no murders, thefts, gross wickednesses of the flesh to own to, ere you pass to God's assize?"

"A few throat-cuttings, holy Father, only a few," smoothed Clement;"I do assure you the Church lays major stress on what we have acknowledged, and time now presses."

Jerome swept his hands about in fearful anger.

"*'Depart from me, ye cursed, into everlasting fire, prepared for the Devil and his angels.'* When I absolve such as you let Satan possess my soul with yours!"

"You will not?" shrieked Michael, leaping up and waving the axe.

"No, since I fear God!"

The Wartburg shook with the bursting of the last barrier. They heard a whooping war-shout.

"An end to this folly," cried Ulrich, his sword leaping forth;"kill him first, then go out fighting, whether St. Michael or Beelzebub snatch us."

Jerome never blinked. They cursed, raved, but he was silent. Now feet trampled in the court. Priest Clement grew grey with fear, but he swung an axe too.

"*Absolvo! Absolvo!* Say but the word," he screamed, and buffeted Jerome, who stood like a stony tower, silent, but frowning terrible.

"Kill him! Curse him!" cried Clement;"they are on us, and we are burned forever."

But high above the groan of the hunted and the shout of the hunters sounded the Graf's voice:—

"For the love of Christ! Hold!"

CHAPTER IX
HARUN KNOWS THE WAY

BEFORE the dawn the moon had gone down; the twinkling stars only made the vast night blacker. A wind was tumbling the forest boughs till they clashed and groaned like the spirits of lost souls. The fox was crouching in his covert, the sleepy redbreast in his hollow peered forth once to see if the dawn were near,—only blackness in the east, and the bird again hid his drowsy head. Yet there was life in the forest,—a living thing was moving. Here the twigs snapped; there a thorn-bush crackled. A deer was roving, or what else? Had any eyes pierced through the dark, they might have seen a form—a human form—thrusting across the thickets. Witch Martha seemed to need no eyes; if eyes she had, they were those of an owl or of an angel who saw the hidden things of the night. On her shoulders sat the two ravens, and once when she stumbled over a rotted bough the twain croaked out together, but she bade them"silence" in so sharp a voice that Zodok and Zebek kept their wisdom shut within their heads. Once Martha's little body ceased its gliding, and she laid her head down to the ground and listened."I can hear it,—the gushing of the stream.

I approach the Dragon's Dale."

Then with surer motion she went onward. Soon the leafy roof was breaking overhead. She saw the stars blink down at her. There was a clearing, and the traced outlines of a tiny hut. And Witch Martha stopped and looked about her.

No glow of embers from the door; no stir of human life. The long boughs above moaned out her only welcome. But of a sudden there was a stealthy footfall from the thicket, and then a whining cry, low and plaintive as a child in pain, but ending with a wild and brutish wail; and Martha turned quickly toward the sound, whilst the two ravens flapped and cawed again.

"Harun!" cried Martha; and again in answer came that wail. Then a dark form slipped out of the covert, a damp muzzle sniffed at Martha's hands, into her face peered two great coals of fire,—the great wolf's eyes,—and Harun whined with his delight.

"Gone; he is gone," spoke Witch Martha."They have borne St. Jerome to the Wartburg, and the little lady—she is vanished too." To which Harun whined yet more.

"And you are lonely, and have sought for him in vain?" Another whine."And he is in peril, and war rages round the Wartburg?"

The wolf stood waiting, wagging assent with his tail. Then Martha changed her voice."Hark, Harun, we must find the little lady." He gave back a bark."You must show me the way. You must sniff at this." And she held to his muzzle something white."Do you understand? Yes?" for Harun's bark was knowing now."You will lead the way; I will follow. We will find the little lady together."

Well that Martha had the airy elves or some other potent

sprites to aid. Over thorn and bush, over dale and hillock, led
Harun, now swift, now slow. Once he missed the scent, and
whined hard till he found it. When he reached the spot where
Agnes had cried out the former night he stopped; but Martha
would not let him stay. Weariness, darkness,—what were
they to fright her? Then he found the way to the deserted
garden, just as the first glimmer of pale dawn spread over the
Thuringerwald, and presently Harun held his mouth close to
the ground, and gave a little cry different from any before.

"Another in the forest? Some one has joined the little
lady? It is so?"

Thus Martha; and Harun answered with another cry.
Then he shambled off so rapidly, that his comrade, swift and
cat-footed as she was, might scarce keep up with him. Now
the grey dawn burst into red gold, and the gold turned into
fire. Now the bird-song woke in the forest, and the strong
breeze sank to a dreamy whisper, as if to lull to the last fond
sleep ere the waking. The great beech avenues spread off
into dimming vistas, and through their midst peered out the
purple-breasted hills. But Witch Martha only looked before
her keenly, and said within her sly old breast:—

"As I feared,—to the Rothensteinand the hold of Fritz the
Masterless. What now is best? Back to the Lord Graf, and ask
him for men? But in that time there is room for many a deed."

Hereupon Zodok shook his glossy wings and cried:—

> "Good Christians, look out!
> The Devil's about!"

"Ay," quoth his mistress;"for Fritz is no small devil, and
Dame Gerda is one greater,—the less cause to leave a dove

inside their cage."

And now her feet ran swift beside those of Harun.

Then before them, tawny, steep, the Rothenstein reared clearly, and in front a thin, grey vapor of rising smoke. Whereat Witch Martha halted, and her finger warned Harun that he lag behind. Soon this was the song which Fritz the Masterless and Wolf heard whilst they placed the kettle before the cave. At first they thought only the trees were crooning; then that the thrushes talked. Then their stout knees knocked together, and they began to mutter a prayer to good Saint Anne.

> "I have come down the moonbeam's path soft veering,—
>   Forth! forth,—from your bat-black den!—
> On the wings of the night-doves silent steering,—
>   Swift! swift,—ere I call again!
> Oh, woe to the peasant,—oh, woe to the knight!
> To the lad or the lass who my summons may slight.
>
> "I have tethered my car with the spider's glister,—
>   Forth! forth,—for my weirds are fleet!—
> Its driver skilled was the wood-moth's sister,—
>   Swift! swift,—come my goblin's feet!—
> Oh, 'twere wiser to win the elf-king's spite
> Than that lad or lass should my summons slight!
>
> "I have learned the lore which the wild owl whistles!
>   Forth! forth,—for my mercy dies!—
> I have wove me a dress from the silk of thistles!
>   Swift! swift,—see my sprites arise!—
> Oh, the hawk's grey wing or the sable of night
> Shall not save nor hide, who my summons slight!"

Now Fritz the Masterless would have faced with a stout heart an old bear or three men; but to hear such a singing from the wood was a sore test for any Christian. Likewise young Wolf who stood at his father's side let the crossbow clatter out of his hands almost into the fire. And when they saw the black figure of Witch Martha—the redoubtable woman whom half of Thuringia knew had Baalberith, Behemoth, Elimi, and divers other lively devils at her constant beck—only the saints kept their hair from rising. Such an hour! such a song! such a spell on them already! The two stared at her with wide-open mouths and eyes.

Martha came straight on, gliding—never walking. She approached the fire and the twain. Upon the turf from right to left she drew a circle with her staff around them. Then she spun about on one foot till their wicked eyes grew dizzy watching her. When halting suddenly she looked on Fritz the Masterless, who blurted out a blunt question as to her errand, and grew of a sudden tongue-tied; whereat Witch Martha answered in a chant that made Fritz and Wolf helpless as young calves.

> "The maiden ye hold,
> In evil hands bold
>> Release her, release!
> Or, by every spell
> In heaven or red hell,
>> Your bating breaths cease.
> "The efreets of night,
> The angels of light,
>> Have laid the command;

From the Dawn-spirit's hall,
At the Dragon-prince's call,
I am sent, I am sent,
Agnes, maid, to demand!"

Had the witch's voice power to freeze their breasts to ice? Fritz's hand twitched on his hunting-knife. A flash from Martha's eye—it sank palsied from the hilt. But Wolf was stouter hearted than his sire. So much good silver from Jew Mordecai lost? Not without one struggle. As a doe poises for the bound he made to leap from the charmed circle, but his captor's glance was too quick. He hesitated, was lost. For Martha's hands flew in mystic passes, the two ravens screamed together, and the enchantress sang:—

"Cross the line, the fiends are waiting;
Death is sure, none shuns the fating
Writ up large on high!
Either now obedient bending
Soon afar Maid Agnes sending
Or thou'lt doom-struck lie."

Then her hands twirled swifter, and now Wolf felt the chills within his marrow.

"Moment, moment, swiftly gliding,
Mortals' woe or weal deciding,
Never slack'ning nor abiding,—
Thou shalt tell how chance shall fly!"

"Ho, Gerda!" called Fritz, ready to give a thousand *bezants* (if he had had them) to loose those fetters unseen;"bring out Maid Agnes, and quickly, in Our Lady's name."

He hoped the mention of that blessed name would rob the witch's eyes of their power, but that desire was vain. Forth ran Gerda and the girls, but the latter shrank back into the hut a-shivering. Gerda was of bolder stuff. She tried to brave out Martha's gaze, to parley, question, and refuse to give the prisoner; for even she was not bold enough to deny that they held the maid. But her shrill tongue tripped, her proud front fell, and she grew chill also at the witch's new singing:—

> "Woman bold, I see them flutter,
> Now they menace, now they mutter,—
> Elf and goblin round thy head!
> Witless wight, thine eyes are holden,
> Thou see'st not the silk-spells moulden,
> Woven with the shuttles golden,
> By which captive thou'lt be led."

Then Witch Martha went on to sing of other awful things right on the edge of happening, if Dame Gerda stopped to bicker longer. And the goodwife whimpered out that—

"They were poor folks, had meant no ill, and had found the little lady in the forest. Let the good mother take her, with their blessing, and unloose the spell."

But here right from the hut ran Agnes,—fearless, glad, and flew to Martha with wide-open arms. The witch laughed once,—a laugh that made Dame Gerda sure the two ravens were a pair of fiends, very anxious for her own and her children's souls. Then the sorceress moved about the circle, drawing the staff from left to right, and so lifting a great load also from Fritz's and Wolfs blank minds. She took Maid Agnes by the hand; the ravens cawed again. She flourished thrice on high, and they saw her vanishing in the forest. But, even when hid, her song pealed clearly:—

"Up away! the wood-thrush calls us,
Over ash and beech and thorn!
Up away! the king-oak calls us,
Singing with his leaves to morn.
For the wind-lord wakes,
Through the greenwood shakes
All the trees,
In his glees
As he greets the fire-kissed dawn!

"Swift away! the west wind bears us
Over mount and dale and hill.
Swift away! the flower-breath bears us
Where the bees their sweet stores fill.
For the wood-queen wakes,
And her rose-crown shakes,
Laughing clear,
To my ear,—
For her trilling lips are a bubbling rill!"

* * *

"Dear Martha," said Agnes, "what did you do to Fritz

and to Wolf and to Gerda? By your songs could you really turn them into stone or give them to the gnomes and to the brownies?"

Martha perked her head and answered:—

"Ah, little lady, whether I could or I could not, those three *thought* I could, and by the lizard's spawn" (at which uncanny oath Agnes herself grew creepy),"it is what men and moles think, not what things are, that makes all the rift betwixt popes and peasants."

"Dear Martha," said Agnes, sorely troubled,"say that you really do not have friendship with the Devil."

"Friendship little, but acquaintance;" yet here the smile which spread on Witch Martha's face grew tremulous, she stood stock still, took the little maid in her arms, and kissed her."Oh! may you never know! Oh! may you never lose! Oh! may you always see the brightness of Our Lady's heaven, and forget that the dear God beside His mercy has His wrath!"

"What are you saying?" The child looked perplexed.

"Foolishness!" spoke Martha; but her little body shook with one long sigh."Ah, little one, I have frighted you. But I will never fright you more. So be comforted, for, by Our Blessed Lord, I have never set eye on gnome nor efreet nor devil. Only I use the wit that heaven sends, and by its aid I saved you. And now hearken to strange news."

Then she told Agnes how the Wartburg was beset by her father; of the sore plight of Jerome; and how they must make all haste to reach the besiegers ere the last attack,"lest the holy Jerome become a saint in heaven in sorry deed."

Agnes did not weep when she heard of Jerome's danger.

"He must not die yet," was all she said;"for I heard him

praying and saying that I was a temptress sent from Satan. He must never go up to visit the dear God and tell Him that." And for a while Witch Martha found her feet too slow for those of the child.

They threaded the forest, not in the circling blind mazes which Agnes had followed when alone, but in the straight path which Harun found for them, and it was not long before they heard the brooklet brawling, and Agnes clapped her hands.

"The hut, the stream, and the Dragon's Dale! The dear Dragon's Dale!"

But they might not tarry, and Martha saw with joy that the red banner of Ulrich still was flying above the Wartburg. "Not too late!"

Again they plunged into the greenwood, but now by familiar paths. Agnes's feet were heavy now, but she did not falter. Presently there was a clatter of armour, and tall men-at-arms in plated hauberks stood across their path,—an outpost of the besiegers.

"Who comes!"

But when Witch Martha declared who her companion might be, and when the soldiers saw that the maid was indeed of their own master's face and eyes, and that her dress, though torn, was that of a great lady, the dapper Freiherr, their young chief, swept his plumed cap across his knees in knightly homage, and the shout flew up the slopes of the Wartburg, through all the assailants' camp:—

"Found! found! found! the little lady, the Grafin!"

Then how Graf Ludwig turned from the attack, with his feet almost in the castle court, there is no need to tell.

CHAPTER X
THE EVENING LIGHT

WHEN the attackers moved once more on their prey they entered the great court of the Wartburg, and never a sword flashed forth to halt them. But as Freiherr Gustav at their head bade his men scatter through dungeon and attic, to drag the victims forth, lo! he and the three hundred at his back halted, then stood awed and reverent, as the figure of Jerome of the Dragon's Dale moved to meet them. Then some doffed their basinets, some even fell on their knees, but all besought his blessing, for they knew that here was the saint of the Thuringerwald. And Freiherr Gustav, bowing the knee, with loud voice thanked Our Lady and Her Blessed Son who had released from sorest peril this holy man; then vowed to Jerome that his late oppressors should shortly have foretastes of their everlasting gehenna. But Jerome stayed him with a sign, forbidding the doing of this reverence.

"For I have come to confess mine own great fault when I cried to you to destroy this Ulrich and his men. I have heard by your glad shouts that Agnes the maid is found, and in the respite whilst you tarried, the Spirit of God, speaking from my mouth, has touched these despairing sinners, and they will submit themselves to you, expecting no mercy from man, but trusting even at the eleventh hour to the abundant mercies of God. Therefore I command you to be exceeding pitiful unto them, and let him that is guiltless himself cast the first stone against them."

Now this exhortation to compassion Freiherr Gustav loved little; but who could say "no" to a living saint? So he ordered Jerome to be escorted down the slope to Ludwig, at whose mercy any captives lay; while the Freiherr's men soon haled out Ulrich and Michael, Franz and Clement, and the four were speedily roped, and shiveringly awaiting the result of the holy man's embassy. Jerome found the Graf before a splendid tent, with pages and squires about him, himself, in his silvered hauberk, the tallest and proudest of them all; but nestled against his side, tattered, mud-stained, dishevelled, happy, stood Agnes the maid. When she saw Jerome she forgot that he had prayed to be delivered from her tempting. She gave the coo of a dove beholding its long-sundered mate, and ran to him, and he, never asking whether he staked his soul or not, reached down to her, closed his arms on her, and kissed her red mouth seven times. Some smiled, a few nigh laughed, a few nigh wept, but no man thought Jerome the less a saint. Then when Agnes saw so many eyes upon her she grew scared, and fled into the tent; but the great Graf himself had bended the knee before Jerome.

"Holy Father," spoke Ludwig; and he lifted his plumed casque, so that the hermit could look fairly upon his proud, strong, bearded face. "Holy Father, you have saved from death or worse my only child. Florins or fief-lands you do account as vanities, or I would proffer them. Yet what shall be your reward? Shall I give doles to two thousand poor at Goslar? Shall I set crucifixes at three hundred cross-roads? Shall I give Saint Michaelis of Hildesheim pyx, chalice, and candlestick of pure red gold?"

"None of these things, though all such works are holy," answered Jerome; yet as he spoke, and gazed upon the Graf, in some strange manner he seemed all unstrung, so that some whispered darkly, "Ulrich has tortured him." But still he looked on Ludwig with wide, heart-searching eyes; and as he looked the chief was marvellously troubled also.

"None of these things," spoke Jerome, as if compelling speech by force of will; "if gratitude is mine, let my reward be this,—the lives of Ulrich and his crew, that they may be yet changed from Children of Wrath to Children of Obedience."

But here My Lord Graf was very sore displeased. One could see the purple veins in his high forehead swell, and through his haughty lips sped forth an oath,—yet in no Christian tongue,—a cry to some foul jinn of the East. Then to his great amaze Jerome staggered as though a sling-stone smote him.

"Catch him! He faints!"

So cried the Graf, outstretching a strong arm, and many ran, but the hermit rose in stately pride. Next in that same strange Orient speech he addressed Ludwig, and the proud chief in turn startled.

"Invoke no paynim fiends but answer. Have you been long in the East?"

"Yes." But in turn Ludwig gazed as do men when turning mad, while two squires, not understanding the tongue, crossed themselves, fearing their lord was wantonly angering the saint.

"How long?"

"Five years at Acre, two at Antioch, three years a prisoner at Hems."

"That was a long time since?"

"I have been in Europe now fourteen years."

Jerome was staring harder than ever, and all men grew more frighted. Why did he press the Graf so fiercely? Why did the Graf tremble as he answered?

"And you say your name is—"

"Ludwig of the Harz;" but again the Graf winced, and the wondering bystanders knew not what to hope or what to fear. They saw Jerome's stern face growing all grey and pale, yet still he questioned.

"You were three years a prisoner at Hems, then returned direct to Germany?"

"No; I searched for my father. I had heard he had entered a convent when I was taken, but I could not find him. He is surely dead."

The Graf was retreating step by step; the hermit followed him. They could see Jerome was nigh to falling, and that his great will bore him up.

"And was that father a man swift to wrath and swift to strike?"

"Yes; but, ah! dear Christ, so was I!" and now the Graf was more ashen than the hermit.

"And did you and your father part in love or hate? Speak for the fear of God!"

"He cursed me. He is dead. At the Judgment Bar he will rise up against me. I cannot bear it. God can forgive me; never he."

Ludwig pressed his hands to his face; his great frame shook.

"Now tell what was your father's true name," commanded the hermit.

"I will not tell!" The Graf nigh screamed it in panic-stricken defiance.

"You *will* tell, and tell it truly, that God may pity you on His last Great Day. What was your father's name?"

"Heinrich of Waldau."

"And your true name is not Ludwig, but—"

"Sigismund." The word was dragged across the Graf's set teeth. But a loud cry rang through the forest.

"Jesu!"

And Jerome lay as one dead upon the greensward.

* * *

Many swore "he is dead," and even the Graf's Padua-trained physician was one of them. But Witch Martha brought him back to breath, though it took small wisdom in leech-craft to know that if he woke at all, it could not be for long. Nevertheless he did wake just as the afternoon shadows were falling in slanting glory across the hill of the Wartburg. Many stood by, hoping to be edified by the last words and moments of a very saint; but Graf Ludwig made a commanding gesture, and all vanished from the tent, saving he. Then he knelt down by the camp-bed, and a tear rolled down the iron cheek of Ludwig of the Harz, to fall on the iron cheek of Jerome of the Dragon's Dale.

"My father."

"My son."

That was all for a very long time; and then Ludwig (for

so men would call him still), that tall strong man, before whom robber-barons trembled, spoke, and his voice was nigh to sobbing.

"Father, father, I have sinned against heaven, and am not worthy to be called your son."

"The fault was mine, Sigismund,—mine."

Thus Jerome, but Ludwig answered him:—

"I was wilful and swift to wrath. I defied you at Antioch when we stood in the room where the form of my sister Agnes lay unburied. I have richly earned your curse. I strode from your presence impenitent. I rode away on the foray to Hems, and was taken prisoner. Amongst the infidels I was once close to winning liberty by renouncing Our Lord. What but the prayers of Mathilde, my sainted mother in heaven, of my angel sister, and of you held me steadfast? I escaped from captivity to hear that you had returned to Europe to bury yourself in a convent. I sought in every abbey in France and Italy, Germany and Spain, to fall at your feet, and crave but the two words, 'I forgive.' Finding you not, I was sure that you were dead, and at the throne of God would rise up, implacable, to accuse me; and your curse is dinning in my ears ever! ever!"

"They told me you were slain before Hems," said Jerome, simply.

"I had disgraced your name. I took another. In the war and wrack, into which Germany fell, I found means of advancement. I married a woman, pure and good, but the wise God soon took her away. She left a little maid. I named her Agnes for my sister. Is she not an angel born?"

"And I dreamed she was a fiend," said Jerome.

"And now, my father, I have prospered mightily. I am

trusted of kaiser and feared of vassal. I have lands, and lieges, and nobly growing fame. But your curse has bittered every sweet; has darkened every sunbeam. Forgive, forgive me, oh, my father!"

Jerome sat upon the camp-bed, and his lips moved in prayer.

"Now God be merciful to me, a sinner."

Then he looked on the Graf, who had bowed his head, whilst tears rained fast.

"I will forgive you, oh, Sigismund, for whose soul I have prayed and striven these many years. For you I have fled the world, the company of men, the love of women, wrestling, toiling, suffering, that I might redeem your soul from the endless death. I will forgive you. But do you first forgive me?"

And then what more they said it is not wise to tell.

After a while Jerome asked of Ludwig:—

"Where is the little maid?" So they brought in Agnes, who cooed and chattered in the great saint's arms, for"saint" she would call him still, though he said he was her grandfather.

"And you will take him away with us to Goslar?" she asked the Graf; "and because he is holy you will set him over the abbey, and he shall dwell in splendid state with chaplains and palfreys, acolytes and squires, like the Lord Prince Bishop of Bamberg?"

Ludwig answered"Yes"; but Jerome only repeated:—

"Chaplains and palfreys, acolytes and squires,—mine?"

Whereat—most marvellous of all the marvels written in this book—the Saint of the Dragon's Dale laughed as brightly as might Maid Agnes herself; and she was very happy. After a while he kissed Agnes again, and grew pensive; yet, as all others listened, Jerome spoke:—

"I am weary, weary. I have waited long. But God is very good, and of the things to come I can fear nothing. I have wrought and fought in North Land and South Land, with paynim, with Christian. Byzantium and Paris, Jerusalem and Bergen, Palermo and Cairo,—I know them all. I have suffered and sorrowed, in pain and in darkness, but at the end, at the end,—" and his face glows with its inborn bright-ness,—"*it shall come to pass, that at evening time there shall be light.*"

* * *

They found him in the morning sleeping. Maid Agnes wept for long. Graf Ludwig was shut within his tent an hour, and went for a month with a face which men had fear to look upon. There was wisdom in plenty, for some said that Jerome had long been suffering of a mortal complaint which only his iron will had battled back, and now that will was relaxed; others, that in excess of joy the mortal cords were loosed; but most, that angels had visited him by night to set him in the burning chariot and bear him up to heaven. Yet all were agreed in saying, "It is well; to-day the bells on high must ring, and all the golden streets be garland-lined, for Christ's strong warrior enters for his crown."

The Prior of Halberstadt who rode with the army fain would have had the holy clay transported to his abbey, there to be cased in gold, and adored by many a pilgrim; but Graf Ludwig answered sternly, "Nay," for he knew his father's heart. Therefore they wound down the Dragon's

Dale,—priests, and lords, and men-at-arms, approaching the hut in the clearing. No sombre procession this; but for the lack of heralds and of minne-singers one might have deemed it a triumph. "Alleluia!" sang many, as they started the red deer in the coppice; and soon all broke forth into praise of Our Blessed Lady, who welcomed her servant home.

> "Ave maris Stella
> Dei Mater alma,
> Atque semper virgo
> Felix cœli porta!"

And the stream as it purled through the Annathal, the birds as they answered the talking pines, the wind as it crooned over the green sea of the Thuringerwald,—all swelled the echoing chorus,—

> "Alleluia! Alleluia! Alleluia! Amen!"

Graf Ludwig strove to penetrate Witch Martha's secret when he thanked her for the service done his child. Would she not come to Goslar? Would she not forsake her uncanny art and be a nurse and governess to the little Grafin? She had only refusals. She would tell nothing of her life-story,—which Ludwig guessed must have been a strange one,—she would not quit the forest. She only accepted a little gold "that she might not vex him."

"The greenwood covers many a secret, and let it cover mine," was her answer.

So she kissed Maid Agnes twice, and with Zodok and

Zebek a-croaking on her shoulders vanished under the trees. Harun gave one regretful howl above a new grave, and trotted after. Nor did Agnes ever see the witch again.

As for Ulrich and Franz, Michael and Clement, they solemnly swore to go immediately to Rome and perform any penance commanded by the Holy Father, and the Graf sent them on their way (first smiting off their thumbs to keep them from temptation); but whether they ended in heaven or elsewhere is known best by the recording angel. However, Freiherr Gustav, whom Ludwig left in the Wartburg, warned perchance by Martha, pounced on Fritz the Masterless full soon, and hanged him and Dame Gerda high—thus proving that ravens bear ill luck, and also leaving two less sinners in an overwicked world.

As for Maid Agnes,—"Maid" no more, but"The Most Gracious Grafin,"—she became a great lady in the North Country. Still, though she grew worldly-wise, stately, and the wife of a very duke, every year she went on pilgrimage to a certain shrine near Eisenach. And if any one marvelled at her piety, her daughters always said:—

"Our mother came rightly by her holiness; her grandfather was a true-born saint."

Thus, for many years, until the pillage and sack of the Peasants' War, the good folk of Thuringia went on pilgrimage to the little shrine under the talking tree in the Dragon's Dale, and to their prayers failed not to add,"*Sancle Hieronyme Eisenacha, ora pro nobis.*"

IN THEIR OWN WORDS
(from the 1903 edition)

MR. WILLIAM STEARNS DAVIS, the author of"A Friend of Caesar,""God Wills It," and"The Saint of the Dragon's Dale," was born on April 30, 1877, at the home of his grandfather, President William Stearns of Amherst College. His father is William V. M. Davis, who for many years has been pastor of the First Parish Church of Pittsfield, Mass. Before coming to Pittsfield, Mr. Davis, Senior, ,was pastor of the Euclid Avenue Presbyterian Church of Cleveland, O.; and the author of" God Wills It" spent his boyhood in that city. From both his father and his mother he inherited literary tastes, and he has always lived in the atmosphere of books.

It was his fortune, good or bad, to be shut out from the normal boy-life, from the age of ten to eighteen, by a sickness that baffled the physicians. During these years of imprisonment, however, he learned to forget his pain by historical reading, and, later, by trying to write for himself histories and historical romances. His father preserves some seven thousand pages of manuscript written before the boy was eighteen. During the years before he entered

Harvard he wrote six historical novels, none of which has ever seen the light of day, or ever will. At the age of eighteen a new physician discovered and removed the cause of his sickness. Immediately the boy's ambition arose; and he fitted himself, in about eighteen months, to enter Harvard College. His schooling had been much interrupted by illness and invalidism, but his mind was so keen and active that when he was able to study, he more than made up for lost time.

Entering Harvard when he was twenty, he graduated in 1900, at the age of twenty-three. He not only went through in three years, which is a rare feat, but he also attained such high rank in his class that he was the first drawn for the Phi Beta Kappa, in a class of nearly five hundred men. In particular he distinguished himself in historical studies; but he made no attempt at writing for publication, beyond a few bits of verse, until his sophomore year at Harvard.

During that year he wrote his first novel, "A Friend of Caesar." He gathered the materials and compiled the outline for the book while too ill to pursue legitimate consecutive studies. The book was actually written as a *jeu d'esprit* and without thought of publication. It was immediately received as a remarkable attempt to reconstruct ancient life. After graduating, he stayed another year at Harvard; and while thus gaining his master's degree, he wrote his second book, "God Wills It," a vivid picture of European society at the time of the First Crusade. His first book established him at once as one of the writers who are trying to do something worth while, and who are worth consideration. Primarily, he desired to write an interesting story. Secondarily, he tried to render lucid certain phases in ancient society and to show the development of character and the true greatness of Julius Caesar. Besides this, he wished to make the classical atmosphere somewhat less vague and impracticable than it is to a great many people, even cultivated people, to-day.

The year following his last at Harvard was spent largely in European travel, during which, however, he found time to write a third story. Like his others, it dealt with life at a time very remote from the present. The new novel upon which Mr. Davis is now working, by the way, pictures the life of Athens at the era of its greatest glory, about the year 440 B.C. Many of the famous men of Athens at that time enter into the book, which has for hero a typical young Athenian. As in the case of many bright men who have not enjoyed good health, Mr. Davis is essentially a student and a scholar. (It is his plan, by the way, to return to Harvard this fall to complete his studies for the doctorate.) Yet his interest in the eras of which he writes is first of all concerned with their human elements. Who the people of those days were, how they lived and thought and acted, what they moved toward, and what they believed and aimed for, constitute his chief interest in them. His style is good; his narrative is always clear; his plots, though containing plenty of elements to afford variety, are never so complicated as to be confusing. His readers find that peculiar unconscious enjoyment which comes from a book wherein the author has had something to say and has said it well.